THE X BAR X BOYS
IN THUNDER CANYON

BY
JAMES CODY FERRIS

I0626439

"IN HER HAND THE WOMAN HELD A LONG BARRELED RIFLE"

The X Bar X Boys in Thunder Canyon.   Frontispiece

THE X BAR X BOYS
IN THUNDER CANYON

BY
JAMES CODY FERRIS

Originally published in 1926.

Published by Wildside Press LLC
Visit us online at wildsidepress.com

CHAPTER I

The Landslide

Raising his head in a gesture of disdain that was almost human, the horse walked stiff-legged around a porcupine that lay in the center of the trail.

"Steering clear of needles, Flash?" said his rider, laughing cheerfully. "Say, Roy," he called to his companion, who sat astride a chestnut mustang, "is it true that porcupines can shoot their quills?"

"Bunk!" answered Roy Manley briefly. "Pure bunk, Teddy. You don't mean to say you believed that, do you?"

"Well, now, that's a question," Teddy Manley replied, a veiled twinkle in his eyes. "Some say one thing, some say another. Pop Burns told me a porcupine shot him full of quills from ten feet away."

"Pop Burns!" Roy snorted. "He could convince an Eskimo that ice was made of rock candy. You ought to know Pop by this time."

The two brothers pulled their horses to a halt and gazed curiously at the small, quilled animal. The boys were alike in build, both being lean, wiry products of ranch life. Teddy Manley, fifteen years old, one year younger than Roy, had light hair and blue eyes, favoring his mother, Mrs. Bardwell Manley, in these respects. Roy took after his father in the matter of eyes and hair — both of these being brown.

Roy ran his hand over the ears of Star, his pony. From any other, this would have been cause for immediate proceedings tending toward the unseating of the rider, but now Star whinnied affectionately.

"Tell you what," Roy declared. "Let's bring this sticker home with us and get Pop to explain how it shoots its quills."

"Good idea," Teddy answered, grinning. "You're elected, Roy. How are you going to carry it?"

"Humph! Never thought of that," the brother demurred. "If we had something we could wrap it up in —"

"Or if we had a wagon," Teddy went on. He was deriving much amusement from Roy's serious attention to the problem at hand. Quieter, and looking at life through graver eyes than Teddy, Roy would frequently devote himself to the solemn consideration of a question which Teddy would dismiss with a light laugh. Roy's nature was drawn from his mother, who, before her marriage to Bardwell Manley, had been a schoolteacher in Denver.

5

"Why don't you tie him to Star's tail?" asked Teddy, his face a study in innocence.

"Why don't I? A fine suggestion!" his brother burst out. "Why don't you carry him under your arm? You've got a leather vest on — you won't get stuck."

Teddy assumed to consider this proposition. He dismounted and walked toward the porcupine. Bending over, he peered closely at the curled-up animal.

"Looks as if he were dead," the boy said finally.

"He's not dead," Roy declared convincingly. "You try to pat him on the head if you think so. He just curls up so you'll let him alone."

"Like a steam roller?"

"Yea, like a steam roller," answered Roy, with a grin. "If you think I'm going to ask why, you're mistaken. Go on, pick him up, Teddy. He won't hurt you. He likes children."

"Then why don't you take a crack at him?" the other boy demanded. The one year's difference in their ages was a touchy point with Teddy.

"Too busy. I have to hold your horse or he'll slide down the mountain side."

The two boys were returning from a ride across the country. They had been investigating some land that their father, who was the owner of the X Bar X Ranch, was thinking of purchasing for grazing ground. They had stayed longer than they had intended, and, wishing to reach home before night, had taken a short cut over Mica Mountain. The riding was not of the best, especially at this time of year when the warm summer sun had melted the snows on the peaks and the water, flowing down, was loosening the top soil. But the brothers were willing to chance a possible accident for the sake of arriving home "in time for grub."

"Don't worry about Flash!" Teddy exclaimed. "He could stand on the side of a house. Well, what's the news? Are we going to take old Needleback home with us?"

"Sure! Wrap him in —" Roy stopped suddenly. He tilted his head forward in a listening attitude.

"Thunder," Teddy remarked. "I heard it, too. Come on, let's be on our way. Never mind the porcupine." He walked over to Flash and rested his hand on the pommel of the saddle. As he did so the rolling noise was repeated, this time much louder.

"Thunder nothing!" Roy cried. "There's not a cloud in the sky. That's up the mountain some place."

"Well, whatever it is, I don't like the sound of it!" came from Teddy, as he vaulted into the saddle. "Makes my flesh creep. I'm tired, I guess. We've been riding ever since early morning. That's the longest stretch I've been on a horse since that night we chased the rustlers all over creation. Baby, that was *some* time! Wonder what happened to the three men who got away?"

"Oh, I suppose they left the country," Roy answered, as he guided his bronco down the steep trail. "Birds like that don't linger long in one place, especially when they know that place isn't healthy for them. The four we put in jail are there for a good stretch, I hope — though that jail in Hawley isn't any too strong."

"You said it! Well, if they escape, they escape, that's all. But they'd better not try any more funny work around here. Dad'll salivate 'em. Jimminy! I wonder what that noise was that we heard. It's got me kind of leery."

"Rocks falling, most likely. Don't know what else it could be. I know it isn't thunder. Come on, get a wiggle on. Be dark soon. Watch your step, this footing isn't any too good."

Keeping firm hands on the reins, the two ranch boys proceeded down the mountain side. The ground was covered with a loose shale, and the mountain on this side was nearly devoid of trees. It would not do to urge the horses to a faster gait than they naturally took, for a fall here meant a nasty slide.

"I hear Nell and Ethel are going to stay at the 8 X 8 most of this coming winter," Roy remarked casually, as he guided Star around a large rock. He referred to two New York girls with whom the brothers had become acquainted some time before.

"You don't say!" his brother returned, in a bantering tone. "I suppose the news just trickled out! You didn't ask mother to 'phone over to Mrs. Ball and find out, did you? Oh, no! Well, let's have it all. Why are they going to stay all winter, Mr. Bones?"

"Aw, dry up," Roy said, laughing, albeit his face was a trifle red. "Trying to kid me, aren't you? How's Curly, Ted? Have you heard from her lately?"

"No, I haven't!" and Teddy in his turn became flustered. "But I know why they are going to stay all winter, even if you don't. Their folks went abroad. Mr. Carew had to settle an estate with ramifications in Italy, and Mr. and Mrs. Willis went with him and his wife."

"Oh-ho! Our little detective on the job! Say, don't try to kid me. After that you haven't got a word to say! Star, take it easy! This pony must want to get home in a hurry." Roy steadied his grip on the reins.

"Guess he didn't like that noise any more than we did," Teddy suggested. "These horses know almost as much as we do, they've been with us so long. It was sure tough when the rustlers stole them, wasn't it? Great to have them back, though."

7

"I'll tell a maverick it is! And we're lucky those rustlers — especially Froud — didn't ride 'em to death. Checkered Shirt prevented Froud from injuring them, I guess. Wonder what became of him!"

"Can't imagine. He turned out to be a pretty decent sort of a hombre after all, didn't he? Well, I wish him luck. He certainly did us a favor."

Teddy was referring to the leader of a gang of rustlers who had turned friendly when the brothers saved him from death and had in consequence helped them recover their ponies, which had been stolen by Gilly Froud to revenge himself against Mr. Manley for his discharge by the ranch owner.

As the brothers rode down the trail, Roy frequently turned in his saddle and gazed up the mountain. Finally Teddy asked:

"What's the idea, Roy? Why the interested stare? Expect to see a friend of yours?"

"Not any. But I'm still curious about that noise. Seems to have stopped, and I'd like to know what it really was."

"Thought you said it was rocks falling down the mountain?"

"Well, it probably was. But that doesn't prove anything. Suppose it was a landslide? It might be, you know. And landslides aren't things you can fool with."

"A landslide on Mica Mountain? Forget it! Never knew one to happen yet. Golly, look at that buzzard! Wish I had a rifle along; bet I could knock him for a loup."

Roy turned again in his saddle. Evidently he had not heard Teddy's remark about the bird circling overhead, for he did not reply. Instead he listened intently.

"Say, what's the matter with you?" Teddy demanded, as he watched his brother. "You give me the willies. Why don't you —"

Roy held up his hand.

"Listen!" he commanded. "Hear that?"

To the boys' ears came that same queer rumbling noise. Now it did not decrease as it had before, but grew louder and louder. The brothers faced each other, paling beneath their tan.

Suddenly a stone hit the ground with a crash directly in front of Teddy's horse. The thunder increased in volume — it seemed almost at their heels. Then another stone fell — and another!

Like a flash, both boys turned. What they saw caused their breath to stick in their throats and their hearts to beat madly.

The whole mountain side seemed to have been torn loose. Huge boulders were tumbling toward them. The few trees that dotted the landscape were uprooted and toppled with majestic force. The air was filled with flying pieces of rock!

Above all rose that sullen, deep-throated roar like a giant in anger.

CHAPTER II

A MISSING BROTHER

"Ride!" Teddy yelled. "It's a landslide! Watch out for —"

His words were drowned by a *bo-o-o-m!* that seemed to shake the mountain to its very base. Teddy wasted no more time in useless explanations. Wisely he gave Flash his head and let the bronco pick his own path down the treacherous incline.

As horse and rider catapulted toward level ground, Teddy's first thought was for his brother. He turned swiftly in the saddle, and his heart gave a leap when he saw that Roy had disappeared. Frantically the boy peered through the haze of dust which hung over the landscape like a pall, but Roy was nowhere to be seen. Teddy knew it would be hopeless to yell, as he could never make himself heard over the crashing roar of the landslide.

With a silent prayer for his brother's safety, the rider was forced to use all his skill to retain his seat in the saddle. Lucky for him that he had, as his father put it, "been born aboard a bronc," else he must surely have been flung to the ground, to be seriously injured, if not killed, by the rocks and trees that were sweeping swiftly down the mountain side, almost at his heels.

Flash, his eyes white with fright, was leaping for safety like some wild animal. Now and then he would give a whinny of terror as a rock landed at his side with a thud. The chances were about even that the boy and his pony would avoid the falling stones. Yet, as each one hurtled by, it seemed certain that the next must strike and send the horse and rider crashing to the ground.

"Stick to it, Flash!" Teddy panted, drawing his hand quickly over his eyes to clear them of sweat. "Another five hundred feet and we'll be safe — the slide is slowing up! If I could only see — this dust — if Roy is safe —"

The grinding noise to the rear of the boy was gradually lessening, and the hurtling rocks were becoming fewer in number. Still Teddy knew he was by no means safe, as any moment another slide might start and overtake him. And a second slide, piled on top of the already loosened earth, might completely overwhelm him. He must ride, and ride hard, if he wished to place himself out of danger.

Flash's trip down the mountain was one of breath-taking escapes from destruction. Teddy swayed with him as though he were a part of the horse. Almost automatically, the boy would know when the bronco was going to plant his feet to avoid a sudden drop, and he would brace himself for the shock. Then the pony would slide and leap — slide and leap. On Teddy's part it was a marvel of horsemanship; on Flash's part it was a wonderful example of animal intelligence. Frightened as he was, the pony never once made a misstep, never once gave way to his terror and dashed blindly forward. Had he done so it would have meant the end for Teddy Manley.

At this moment the young rancher bore little resemblance to the young man registered as "Theodore Havens Manley, Latin Scientific Course," on the records of the Hopper Boarding School. His face was streaked with dust, and perspiration had smudged it into a black mask. His hat was gone — swept off by a swishing branch — and his hair was in wild disorder. His clothing was torn in several places by the bushes he had dashed through. He was panting fiercely, and his eyes were sharpened into two points of blue light. From his lips came words that were barely articulate.

"Now, Flash — watch that rock! Stick to it, old boy, stick to it — a little more — yow! That was a close one! All right, baby, you're not hurt — take it easy now — "

A leap — a swift, neck-jerking halt — slipping, sliding, trying desperately for a foothold — another leap —

Suddenly a yell burst from Teddy's lips. Frantically he pulled on the reins, seeking vainly to stop the pony almost in midair. The boy's face paled. In front of him, so close that the horse's forefeet seemed on the very edge, yawned a deep gully!

"Flash! We're done for! Ah-h — "

In the second that remained to him Teddy made his decision. It was impossible to stop, the gully seemed to rush eagerly to meet them. There was only one chance — that Flash could clear it, could leap to the other side.

Teddy released the reins. He dug his heels deep into the pony's sides. And, with his heart in his throat, the boy felt the horse rise beneath him and sail through the air.

For a moment the mount and his rider were silhouetted against the sky like a frantic picture thrown on the silversheet. A moment — then Teddy felt his very bones grind together in the shock of that swift descent. Vaguely he looked about him. Flash, trembling like a leaf, was standing upon a broad plateau. They were safe!

Teddy nodded his head several times, slowly, deliberately, as if to confirm his past thoughts. Then he dismounted stiffly, and putting a hand on either side of the pony's head, he looked him straight in the eyes. For a second — perhaps two — he stood there, while Flash gradually grew still and breathed easier. When he whinnied softly, Teddy rubbed the pony's ears and stepped back.

"Finish!" the boy said. Then he laughed, adding:

"Me, I'm going to join the aviation and have you for a plane! Jimminy, what a jump! Let's see — "

Turning, Teddy walked to the edge. The dust of the landslide had almost settled, and he saw plainly the other side of the gully. It was a great deal higher than the land on which he stood, which difference in elevation was the only reason Flash had been able to make the leap. No horse could have jumped that distance on the level. Even with this drop to aid him, it seemed almost impossible that Flash had done it. Yet there he stood, looking at his master with knowing eyes, and here Teddy stood — safe!

"But where in thunder *am* I?" the boy exclaimed suddenly. "I don't remember seeing this gully before. If I could get to the other side again I could probably find my way home, but there's not a dog's chance of ever leaping back." He looked down into the abyss and shuddered. The thought of that tremendous jump was unnerving.

As Teddy walked toward Flash, he felt a wave of uneasiness pass over him, as though an unpleasant thought were hiding in his brain somewhere. His mind leaped forward.

"Roy!"

Where was his brother? What had happened to him? Did he escape? They were both ahead of the slide, surely he could not have fallen! Star could bring him out of it — unless he was struck by a rock!

Teddy hunched his shoulders. He ran his hand through his hair and discovered for the first time that he had no hat on. Then he looked about him, as if he expected to find the hat lying under a bush. The hat — never mind the hat! Roy was gone!

In silence and with a deep frown creasing his forehead, Teddy remounted. Could it be possible that his brother had come to this same gully and, as he had, leaped with his horse to the other side? Teddy cast his eye along the opposite edge. Less than a quarter of a mile away the lip of the gorge dipped down, so that it was level with the plateau on which Flash stood. The meaning of this struck Teddy like a dash of cold water. This, then, was the only place the leap could be made! If a pony tried the jump where both sides were level, he would hit the cliff with his hind feet, while his front feet would paw desperately on the loose earth of the plateau's edge, seeking madly to draw himself and his rider to safety, then with a scream he would lose his hold — fall backward — turning over and over — over and over —

A groan burst from Teddy's lips.

It could not be! It must not be! Roy was safe! He had turned to one side and had ridden from under the landslide. Now he was looking for Teddy, wondering what had happened, wondering if Teddy had made it all right. Now he was taking off his hat, rubbing back his hair and muttering something about, "I'll tell a maverick that was some ruckus!" Certainly he was safe, Teddy argued. Roy — good old Roy — he'd come riding along any minute now and yell across to his brother asking him if the landslide didn't remind him of the scene in "The Fall of Pompeii."

But Roy did not come riding along, and the sun was casting long shadows as Teddy rode slowly along the edge of the gorge. Somehow he would have to find his way out of here. He must reach home and send a party out to search for Roy. No, Roy would be waiting for him when he got there! Maybe he would arrive in time to halt those who were about to start after Teddy. If he hurried they might find Roy before it was too late! No, no! Roy was home already!

"Can't go on like this," the boy muttered, bending low over the pony's head. "The thing to do is to find dad as quickly as I can and tell him. He'll know what to do. But I won't let mother know — not until we find Roy. Then Roy can tell her. If I could only remember this gully I might reach the ranch without riding all over the landscape."

He hunched his shoulders again, as another boy might straighten up, and thrust his chin forward. Chirping to his mount, he increased his pace.

The sky above him had turned to a pale blue that was almost white, while to the west, beyond the mountains, a riot of color blazed. Teddy threw his head back as a shrill, hoarse cry of a circling buzzard tore the silence. Then the boy raised in his stirrups and shook his fist fiercely at the winged carrion-eater.

"What do you want here? There's nothing for you! Search! Go ahead and search, you filthy buzzard! You won't find anything, I tell you! Roy is home — home! And he and I will come out to-morrow and toss some lead into you! Maybe you'll like to try that for a change of diet!"

Strangely enough, the bird ceased his ominous circling, and with another scream disappeared over the rim of trees. Teddy sank back into the saddle, his face somewhat red, ashamed of his outburst.

"Must be getting woozy," he muttered. "Yellin' at a buzzard! Never did that before. I wonder — ".

Suddenly he stopped, pulling the reins taut. Above him, outlined against the eastern sky, was the figure of a man on horseback. As he rode closer, a red beam from the setting sun shot through the trees and illuminated his face like a spotlight. Teddy gave a yell.

"Nick! Nick Looker! Yo-o-o, Nick! How do I get out of here? Where's Roy? Hey-y-y, Nick!"

CHAPTER III

THE SLOUCHING RIDER

Nick Looker's answer winged down on the evening breeze.

"Yo-o, Ted! What you say-y-y? Where you been?"

"How do I get out of here?"

"South! Keep south! Straight out from the gully! Then bear west! I'll meet you!"

With a throb of sudden hope in his heart that Nick had found Roy, Teddy turned Flash about and rode rapidly in the direction Nick had indicated.

While the boy is hurrying to meet the young puncher on the trail above him, a few moments will be taken to tell something of Roy and Teddy Manley of the X Bar X Ranch.

The two brothers had been born on their father's ranch, and, with the exception of the three years they had spent at the Hopper Boarding School, just outside of Denver, they had lived the rugged life of the cowboy. Although their father was more than moderately well off, he, as a Westerner of the old school, determined that his boys should have every chance the West offered them to grow into hardy men. Hence it was that they were an important part of the "working crew" on the X Bar X.

As related in the first book of this series, called "The X Bar X Boys on the Ranch," Roy and Teddy succeeded in obtaining information which led to the capture of a band of rustlers at the very moment they had planned to steal cattle from the Manley range. Among these men was Gilly Froud, who was despised even by his cronies because of his cruelty to horses and his mean, avaricious spirit.

It was this coward who, out of revenge for a fancied wrong done him by Mr. Manley, had stolen General, Star, and Flash, the especial horses of Mr. Manley, Roy, and Teddy. That theft was his undoing, for the two boys and their father were determined to recover their favorite mounts at all costs. The many exciting adventures which led to their recovery and the jailing of most of the rustlers, are told of in the book preceding this.

With this explanation, let us return to Teddy as he is riding to meet Nick Looker, a cowboy of the X Bar X outfit.

Following Nick's instructions, the boy bore south out of the gully. Then, in a moment, he spotted a well worn trail, and, practically of his own accord, Flash made for this at a gallop.

"Right under my nose and I couldn't see it!" Teddy murmured bitterly. "What a fine Westerner I am! If I had found this sooner I'd be almost home by now and we could have started after Roy that much quicker. There's just a chance that Nick saw him — just a chance. Baby, I sure hope he has!"

Eager to set his mind at rest, he touched Flash impatiently with his heels. The horse, who was doing his best over the rough ground, turned his head as if in reproach. Teddy grinned slightly.

"All right, ole hoss," he said. "Go ahead. Don't mind me. Guess I'm kind o' nervous. But you can't blame me now, can you?"

At that moment, when Teddy was most concerned over his brother's safety, Roy was within a quarter of a mile of him, across the gully, himself riding toward Nick Looker.

When the landslide came, Roy, realizing his danger, had snapped Star into action with a sudden yell. The next moment the pall of dust hid everything, and Roy had to give his safety into the keeping of his pony.

Star did not fail him. Taking a direction at right angles and to the left of the route Flash had picked, the bronco sought to avoid the rumbling slide by long, desperate bounds. Somehow, he had chosen the only avenue of escape left to him. As he shot over the mountain, Roy noticed that they were leaving the landslide behind. In a few moments he and Star stood in safety, while in the distance the rocks still crashed down the slope.

As Teddy's first thought had been for his brother, so now Roy hoped fervently that Teddy had succeeded in riding clear.

He stopped and looked about him. The thunder of the landslide had died to an echo, and Roy knew that within five minutes the earth would settle entirely. Still it would not be exactly safe to ride over that stretch of mountain for some time, as the least disturbance might start another slide.

"Well, if she starts, she starts," Roy said aloud. "I've got to find Teddy! If he's off his horse, he'll want to ride double with me. Guess Star can hold us; hey, old boy? Get along now. Tread easy. Don't go kicking about or you'll have the whole mountain on top of us. All right, mosey!"

Diagonally across the mountain he rode, his eyes narrowing as the sun neared the horizon and Teddy was still missing. Yet, he thought, no news is good news, and Teddy might even now be waiting at the ranch for him.

To the best of his knowledge, the trail he rode led toward the X Bar X. If Teddy was really lost, it would be best to make for home and send out a searching party. One man could do nothing in this trackless, wild country. Turning in his saddle, Roy squinted at the descending sun, now a dull red ball.

"Take it on the run, Star," he said aloud, in a somewhat anxious voice. "Night, she's coming. Want to find out if Teddy got home safe. If not — "

He did not complete his thought, but let the reins hang loosely over the bronco's neck. Star eased into a gallop.

"I suppose we're going right," Roy remarked after a moment. "Seems as though the ranch should be due east. When that slide came, we were —"

Cutting the sentence off sharply, he pulled back on the reins with all his strength. Star slid forward on stiffened legs, reared, and came to rest within a foot of the edge of the gully. From where Roy sat, it appeared that the pony's head hung over the cliff while the horse himself remained on solid land only by dint of clinging to the earth with his tail, or perhaps with his hind feet, to help him. The boy took a deep breath.

"If it's all the same to you, Star, maybe you'd be just as happy a little farther back. Hey? Easy, now — there's no rush. Let's not do anything sudden. Easy! That's the stuff. Whew!"

Pushing back his sombrero, Roy mopped his forehead.

Then he dismounted and walked forward, to part the bushes and investigate the canyon before him.

"She's deep, all right, and wide," he mused. "Not a chance to jump it — here, at any rate. Funny I don't remember this. Well — "

He shook his head jerkily, in the gesture of a person casting an unpleasant thought from him. Walking swiftly to where he had left Star, he remounted and started silently to follow the canyon. Turning from side to side, so that he might not miss Teddy if the boy were in that vicinity, Roy, glancing to the south, away from the gully, gave a start. In the distance, far up the mountain, he could see the figure of a man on horseback.

"Teddy!" he yelled, then the next moment regretted it. That was not Teddy. He rode differently, slouched to one side. Quickly Roy moved out of sight behind a bush and peered through. The man was gone. Roy could not tell whether he had heard his hail or not.

"Jimminy! he looked familiar." The boy was puzzled. "I've seen a rider just like that somewhere. I wonder if — " Then he smiled to himself at the absurdity of it. The rustlers they had captured were in jail at Hawley. That fellow who had wanted to shoot Froud for knifing his friend Brand was certainly behind bars.

"It couldn't have been him up there! Yet that slouch and the queer way he held his shoulders!"

Roy had not known how vividly the picture of that night had been impressed in his memory. The ride to the north fence — the long wait — then the coming of the rustlers with Froud leading them and the others following, among them one with that strange slouch. No, Roy had not consciously marked the peculiarity of that side-riding horseman. Yet now, when he saw one who recalled the scene, he pictured the rider almost as vividly as if he were before his eyes.

Keenly the boy swept the mountain top with his gaze, but the puncher had disappeared. Roy shrugged his shoulders.

"Guess I'll never know," he commented grimly. "But how could it be that rustler when he's over in Hawley playing solitaire in a cell? My eyes must be doing tricks."

Star whinnied softly, recalling Roy from his reverie.

"Thanks, baby," the boy said with a little chuckle. "You're a grand little alarm-clock, I'll tell a maverick! Let's be going."

With the disappearance of the strange horseman, Roy's mind reverted to Teddy with a sickening fear. A frown came to his face and he chirped to Star, who was moving restlessly forward. With a jump the pony went into a gallop.

"Hey, you!" came a sudden call.

Roy jerked his head around in amazement.

"Where you bound for? Eagles, to get the evenin' mail?"

"Nick!"

"Why not?"

A puncher rode into the open and approached Roy. His tanned face wore a broad grin.

"What's yore hurry?"

"Nick! Have you seen Teddy? Is he safe?"

"Sure, he's safe!" the cowboy chuckled. "Safe an' sound. He'll be here in a minute. I spotted him followin' the gully like a lost sheep. Listen! Think I hear him now. Say —"

But Roy waited no longer. With a yell he started Star toward the sound of the approaching horseman. In a moment the two brothers were face to face.

"Teddy! I was afraid you were —"

"I thought you were —"

They both stopped. Teddy thrust out his hand, and, for a brief moment, it met Roy's in a firm grip that spoke of what was in the heart of each. Then Teddy chuckled.

"Quite a show, hey, Roy?"

"I'll tell a maverick! But, Teddy, when the rocks were busting down a mile a minute and roaring like thunder and the dust started to rise, didn't it remind you of — now tell the truth — didn't it remind you of the eruption of the volcano in 'The Fall of Pompeii?' "

Teddy laughed softly, and side by side the two boys rode toward the X Bar X. Nick, whistling softly, led the way. The sun flashed a last blaze of orange and pink as it sank behind the hills.

Far to the rear, on the mountain top, was a lone horseman, his hand shading his eyes, peering intently at the three riders. Silent and immobile as a statue he sat, slouching sideways in the saddle, as though he were discouraged and weary after a long, long ride.

CHAPTER IV

A MESSAGE IN THE NIGHT

At the ranch that evening, there was much talk of the landslide and of how Nick came upon the two boys "wanderin' around within five hundred yards of each other an' each thinkin' the other was settin' on the ground, tossin' little rocks after big ones," which was Nick's way of telling of the incident.

Mr. Manley, the soul of bluff friendliness and humor, laughed until the ends of his long black mustache curled inward.

But Mrs. Manley, she whom the boys and their father often called, half jokingly, half seriously, "the blonde angel of the West," smiled tenderly. Now that the danger was over, she would not worry. Still in her mother's heart was a prayer of thankfulness for the boys' safety. Often had she watched her sons off on a dangerous mission with a laugh on her lips and anguish in her soul, but they never knew that.

Perhaps Mr. Manley suspected, for at times he would gather her in his arms without a word of warning, and in a soft voice ask her if she was sorry she had come out to "this roughneck West where there's nothin' but cyclones an' wild steers an' rustlers."

Then she would lift her face to his, her eyes shining with just a hint of tears — of happiness, and in a moment Mr. Manley's laugh would go booming out into the sunny yard. Seldom would she answer his question. He knew the reply without being told.

Belle Ada, the daughter of the family, she of the dark eyes and wavy black hair, characterized by Sing Lung, the cook, as "Plitty like litta' black jade house-god," was disappointed that Teddy had not brought home the porcupine. Belle was twelve years old, and a fitting partner for Teddy when any joke was afoot.

"We could have had loads of fun with him," she declared. "Golly! Imagine Pop Burns trying to get him to shoot his quills! I know we could have fixed up something, maybe with rubber bands, so when Pop went near him the quills would shoot! Of course I don't say we *cold* have. I just say maybe. But, anyway — "

"Hey, take it easy!" Teddy interrupted. "We haven't got old Needle-back; so what's the use of supposing? You're lucky to have us back at all, Miss Maybe. Do you realize that?"

"Bugs," Belle stated definitely, with that callousness so attractive in sisters of twelve. "I know you and Roy. It 'ud take more than a landslide to put you under. Like that time you went after the rustlers. If I could have come with you, I'll bet none of them would have gotten away!"

"Is that so!" Roy interrupted, getting up from the steps of the front porch, where he had been sitting, and walking toward Belle. "Is that so! How would you work? What would you do? Shoot 'em all? Would you? Would you? Would — "

"Roy Manley, don't you touch my hair! I just combed it! Roy! If you don't stop — "

With a bound, Roy cleared the railing, while Belle stood in mock fury, shaking her fist.

"Come on, Teddy," the departed brother called back. "Let's go see Nick down at the bunk-house. We can't be bothering with children."

With a laugh, Teddy arose and followed his brother.

"We'll see you later," he whispered as he passed Belle. "Think up a good one, and I'll help you."

Approaching the bunk-house, the two boys saw that Nick, Pop Burns, and Gus Tripp were leaning against the side talking — "settling their supper." In the dusk of the evening, they resembled a picture, so quietly did they stand. The cowboy will seldom move unless it is necessary, but at those times he makes up for his former quiescence.

"Greetings, boys," Teddy called softly.

"And to you, great chiefs, the blessing of the harvest moon," came from Gus. "What brings you-all to the abode of the humble?"

"Make talk," Teddy grunted. "Where do you get that 'humble' stuff? Been getting more love letters, Gus?"

"You tell 'em," Pop chuckled. "Pop" was the oldest puncher on the X Bar X. He claimed to have invented the brand of the Manley ranch when the present owner's father first settled it. Thus he felt entitled to a certain consideration from the "youngsters," as he called the other hands. This respect he often sought to enforce by criticizing the rising generation, much to his later dismay. In the words of Nick, they "hopped all over him."

"Never mind about my love letters," Gus responded, grinning. "I guess Nick, here, can tell us all we want to know about love. He's the hombre that writes the 'advice to the lovelorn' in the *Hawley Register*; ain't you, Nick? An' I know where he gets his dope from, too! Me, if I liked Norine as well as you do, I'd marry the girl, that's what I'd do! Yessir!"

"Dry up," Nick growled. Norine was the daughter of Mrs. Moore, a widow, who for many years had been the housekeeper at the ranch house of the X Bar X. Norine was Irish — and pretty. Nick was not the only puncher on the ranch who had fallen a victim to her charms.

19

"Yep, these kids amuse me," Pop chuckled, sliding gently down the side of the bunk-house until he sat upon the ground, when he proceeded to light and fill a pipe. "They sure tickle me! Talkin' about love! Huh! Why, you birds don't know what love means. Me, I had experience. First gal I ever loved was the dar'ter of a bouncer in a drinkin' place over Tacoma way. She was a gal fer yuh! Shoot? That gal could shoot the eye outta a fly at ten paces. That's the reason I didn't marry her. She was *too* good. The next one was —"

"Aw, take a rest!" Nick exploded. "How do you get thataway? Must think you're King Solomon, or somebody! Pop, there's only one trouble with you. You're too verbose."

"Here!" the old man sat upright, startled. "Don't go callin' names at me, Nick, 'cause I won't have it. I'm tellin' yuh now, I —"

"Take it easy, Pop," Roy broke in. "That doesn't mean anything to get sore about. It means you talk too much."

"Oh!" Pop returned, mollified. "I thought it meant somethin' else. Got to be careful these days, with all the youngsters readin' dictionaries. When I was your age, Nick, all my knowledge I got out of Harvey's Encyclopedia an' an almanack containin' the names of every bird, animal an' fish in creation, with a remedy for all ills the flesh is heir to. Yep, an' she stood me in good stead, too. I remember the time —"

"Gettin' late," Gus declared, stretching high. "Got a pack of tobacco, Nick? I'm all out. Say, what you boys been doin' all day? Seems like I heard some talk of a landslide."

"That was us," Teddy said grimly. He told the story of their escape once more, since Nick had not yet repeated it.

"Guess you were glad to be on the backs of Flash an' Star," Gus commented when Teddy had finished.

"I'll tell a maverick we were!" Roy burst out. "Those horses are almost human! Now you take that jump that Flash made, with Teddy on him. I saw the place, and, baby, it was some leap! How many horses could do that? Then when I gave Star his head, as the rocks started to play tag with me, why, he knew which way to go. Brought me right out of it. By golly, I —"

"Guess during the time the rustlers had them broncs you didn't lose any love for 'em, did ya?" Nick remarked dryly. "Well, you're right, Roy. They're sure some horses!"

"Can't tell me different!" Teddy agreed. "Say, Roy, did you let the boys know about that rider you saw on the mountain? Maybe they know who it is."

"What was that?" Gus asked quickly.

"Well, nothing much," Roy answered, "except that I saw a man who looked a great deal like one of those punchers we rounded up when they tried to steal our cattle. As I remember there was one hombre who sat kind of slouched in the saddle — leaning to the left. Any of you recall that?"

"I do," Nick stated definitely. "When he heard that Froud had knifed Brand, he took a pot shot at him, only he missed. Sure, I remember that slouch. But as far as I know he's in the hoosegow at Hawley. There were only three of the rustlers that made a getaway. That waddy who rides leanin' in his saddle we got. Still, I reckon there's more than one side-winder in these parts."

"Guess so," Roy said musingly. He stared up at the sky through which tiny stars were now peeping. "Going to be a nice day to-morrow," he said in a low tone. "Just right for a ride. Maybe — "

"Maybe," Teddy repeated. "Why not? I'll go with you."

"Huh?" Roy came to with a jerk and looked at his brother. "What do you mean — you'll come with me? Do you think you're a mind reader?"

"Sure do," Teddy replied, grinning broadly. "Guessed right, didn't I? You mean to ride over to the 8 X 8 and see Nell and Ethel, don't you? Oh, never mind denying it. Anyway, I'll go along to see that you get there all right. Can't have bogie-mans get my 'ittle brother. No, sir! Would be terrible. Would be awful. Would be — "

"Chuck it," Roy growled, making a pass at Teddy. "If you come along, it's not to save me from any bogie-man. It's for just one thing — to see Curly! Hey, Pop, what about that? You qualify as an expert. What should a man do when he wants to see a girl and she's ten miles off on another ranch?"

"Buy an airship," Pop chuckled. "Then you can make flyin' visits. Pete Ball would be glad to see you comin', I know. He'd maybe climb up on the roof an' wave to you."

"You're all locoed, I think," Teddy said casually. "I'm going in. Got some work to do."

"Yea, work! Going to write a note to Curly because too many people may listen in if you telephone! Do you call that work?" gibed Roy.

"I would not — anything but!" returned Teddy. "The note wouldn't be poetry though," and he grinned at his brother, who was a lover of verse. "Say, Gus," he went on in a different tone of voice, "how's that cow that was sick? Getting better?"

"She's comin' along all right, Teddy," Gus replied.

Mr. Manley gave the charge of the ranch over to the boys on alternate weeks, and this week Teddy was the foreman. He was responsible for the management of the entire business of the X Bar X.

"Don't let her mix with the others until she's entirely well," Teddy went on. "We don't want any more sickness on our hands. Well, see you boys in the morning. Coming in, Roy?"

21

"Not just yet. I want to — "

Roy had been facing Nick while he was talking, and now he stopped suddenly and whirled about. From around the corner of the bunk-house came the clatter of a pony's feet. The five men stood perfectly still, waiting. The rider appeared, flashing through the night like an apparition. His hat was pulled low over his eyes, and Teddy noticed that he rode not straight up, but leaning to the left.

Close to the five punchers he swung. When he got opposite them, he yelled something and tossed a light stick at Roy. Fluttering from the stick was a piece of white paper. The next moment the rider had swept out of sight behind the bunk-house. The beating of his pony's feet upon the hard earth sounded loud, then the noise grew gradually fainter and at last died away in the distance. He went as he had come.

Teddy stooped forward and picked up the stick with the paper tied to it. He walked into the bunk-house and held it under the lamp. The others crowded around eagerly. Teddy spread the paper out. On it were scribbled the words:

"Bardwell Manley:
    "If you press the charge against those men at Hawley you'll
    get yours with interest. Take our advice and let it drop if you
    want to stay healthy. We mean what we say.
                                                "RELTSUR."

CHAPTER V

THE JUMPING BUCKER

The bunk-house lamp illuminated the faces of five very much surprised cow-punchers. Teddy, who was holding the note, turned it over as though the explanation of its strange arrival might be printed on the back.

" 'Pears like we're a gang of hicks," Gus drawled. "Nick, why didn't you stop that guy? Maybe he could have told us when he was appointed postman."

"Why didn't you stop him yourself?" Nick snorted. "You were as near to him as I was. He rode by almost on yore feet."

"Notice anything queer about the way he rode?" came from Pop. The veteran puncher pulled at his pipe calmly and surveyed the men about him.

"Sure!" Teddy answered. "He was slouched to the left, like he was aiming to sweep something up from the ground. Why, say, Roy, he might have been — "

"He might have been and was," Roy returned grimly. "I'll take a bet that he was the same hombre I saw back on the trail!"

"You mean the waddy you thought was one of the rustlers?" Pop asked curiously.

"Yes, that's just what I mean. Of course I didn't get a very good look at him as he flashed by, but he sure looked familiar. What was that he yelled out?"

"Couldn't get it," Nick replied. "Don't matter, anyway. Now about this note. What'll we do with it?"

"Give it to Sing Lung to make a stew out of," Pop suggested ironically. "Or maybe you'd rather frame it? But unless you want to do that, it *might* be a good idea to show it to the boss."

"Go ahead, ride right on," Nick growled. "I'm just standin' here. Roy, you want to take it in to your dad, an' see what he thinks of it?"

"Sure. Let's go, Teddy. Dad's in his room, I think."

At that moment a step sounded at the door, and all turned quickly — more quickly, perhaps, than such an interruption at another time might merit.

"What's this, a meetin' of discontented workers?" a voice asked, and chuckled. "Seems to me you might close the screen unless you *like* bugs."

"Boss!" Gus exclaimed. "Hey, take a look at this, boss! Just came. By pony express, too."

23

"Guy rode up, goin' like a jack-rabbit," Nick began, "an' tossed this here — "

"Just this second," came from Pop. "I was standin' by the door, talkin' to Nick an' Roy an' Teddy an' Gus, an' I was just sayin' that these days ain't like the old days when I fust came here an' invented the X Bar X brand, when all of a sudden, boss, I heered a pony come tearin' toward — "

"What in thunderation?" demanded Mr. Manley, taking the paper Teddy held silently out to him. Quickly his eyes ran over the words. As he read his lips closed together tightly. Then he looked up.

"This ain't a joke?" he asked.

"Not any!" Teddy exclaimed.

"I'll tell a maverick it isn't!" Roy cried. "At least, it doesn't look like one. It happened just as Pop said when he started that speech of his. We were standing at the door, talking, and a rider came out of the dark and threw this at us, tied to this stick. Then he beat it again before we could wink."

For a moment Mr. Manley said nothing. He pulled first one side of his mustache, then the other. Then he put the paper in his pocket, took out a corncob pipe, filled, and lit it.

"Regular Wild West stuff," he remarked slowly, removing the pipe from his mouth. "Deadeye Bill. Well, let him have his little fun. He don't annoy us any."

"What you goin' to do?" Pop asked.

"Me?" Mr. Manley turned to the speaker, a surprised look on his face. "Why, I'm goin' to hit the hay pretty soon. Gettin' kind of late. She's sure some warm out, ain't she? We'll probably have a long Indian summer. Nick, will you see that General is saddled for me early to-morrow? Want to take a ride over Hawley way. Got somethin' I want to tell the sheriff. Well, I'll be gettin' back. Watch out for that door, Gus, or you'll have all the gnats an' millers in the whole state flyin' around in here."

With a glance toward Roy and Teddy, the ranch owner stepped out into the night. Gus chuckled.

"He's some worried, ain't he? They might just as well have written 'Merry Christmas' on that note for all the boss cares."

"The man that tries to buffalo dad has got a mean job on his hands," Roy declared, with a grin. "He'll push that charge now harder than he would have before. Well, I'll tell you one thing. Froud didn't have a hand in this. He knows dad — and with good reason. He'd never send a note like this if he really wanted the charge dropped. He'd know it would be the one sure way of getting dad to force it."

"You're right, Roy," Teddy remarked. "This was written by one of the men that got away. Wouldn't be surprised if old Slouch himself did the job. Must think he's some hot stuff! Well, he'll learn. He sure will. He's young yet."

"Check," Nick agreed, with a laugh. "Teddy, yore dad is one fine man; you know it? Best boss I ever had. I'm sure glad he's not gonna be scared out of puttin' those rustlers in jail for a long stretch. Yessir, I'm fer the boss every time."

"Me too," came from Gus emphatically. "Ever since that day he went into Rimor's place and took a chance on gettin' plugged in the back just to get some information about the stolen horses, I knew he was the man for me. Notice how he took that note? Never batted an eye. They have to come pretty high to stop him!"

"Sure do," Teddy assented. Then he laughed. "I knew dad 'ud take it that way. Now he'll go over to Hawley in the morning just to tell the sheriff to convict those rustlers sure."

"And I'm sure glad of it," Gus declared. "If I can, I'll ride over myself when they get sentenced! The dirty thieves!"

The puncher has small use for rustlers. The labor of raising cows until they are fit to sell cannot be lightly forgotten and the rustler who steals them is hated with the vindictiveness of a man who has seen his hard work go for nothing.

Later, Teddy and Roy strolled back to the ranch house, leaving Pop to explain to unwilling listeners how the mysterious rider had come and gone so quickly.

The boys were tired, as well they might be, and sought their beds early. They roomed together, their beds being in a room facing the east. The sun was their alarm clock, and the next morning they arose and hurried down to breakfast with an idea of riding with their father to Hawley. But they found he had already left.

The business of the ranch occupied the attention of the brothers until early afternoon, and they had little time to talk of the events of the preceding night. Four new horses had arrived at the X Bar X, and both Teddy and Roy were eager to see if they would make good saddle ponies. Of course the boys were bound to their own mounts by ties of real affection, but it was necessary that some additional riding broncos be made ready each year for the fall round-up.

Teddy, upon investigation of the newly arrived animals, declared that while three seemed fair enough, the fourth had a queer look in his eye.

When Nick saw the bronco, he grunted.

"Bad actor," he said. "I know them kind. Send him back. Tell Clews we don't want no tigers on this ranch. When'd the broncos arrive?"

"Little while ago. I kind of hate to send this pony back, though. Look at the chest on him, won't you!"

"Yea, an' did you take a look at his teeth? Made fer bitin', they are. Better send him back than have him take a chunk out of somebody."

"Think he'd do that?" Roy asked.

"Sure do! If you don't believe it, just you fork him — only leave word what kind of flowers you want."

"Well, now, I don't know about that," Teddy said slowly. He walked over to where the horse stood, rubbing against the bars of the corral, and peered into his eyes. "He doesn't look so bad. Nick, I'd like to take a crack at him. Lend a hand with this cinch, will you?"

"Listen, Teddy," Nick remonstrated. "Don't do nothin' foolish. Even if he don't bite, he's a buckin' fool. I'm certain sure of that. Why take a chance?"

"Yes, Teddy, if I were you I'd wait until dad comes back," Roy added. "He may want to return the pony. Don't ride him."

Teddy did not answer for a moment. Then he took a coin from his pocket.

"Heads I do, tails I don't," he said briefly. "Dad won't want to send the bronc back without knowing what he's good for. The only way to find out, so far as I can see, is to ride him. Here she goes."

The boy spun the coin in the air. As it landed, both Nick and Roy bent over it eagerly.

"Heads," Nick reported. "Now watch your step, Teddy. I know you can ride, but I don't want to see you ploughin' a trench in the dirt. I'll get this here cinch strap good an' tight, so the saddle won't sway none."

In silence the horse was made ready. Teddy stood by his side, and at a signal from him, Roy and Nick stood away. Teddy vaulted into the saddle.

The animal stood like a statue. Not a muscle moved. Teddy whipped his hat from his head and "fanned" the pony. And this time he got results. Straight into the air the animal leaped, landing with legs as stiff as boards. But Teddy was ready for this maneuver, and took the shock with his feet firm in the stirrups.

"Stick to him!" Nick yelled. "Watch out that he doesn't swing his head on you!"

The warning came not a moment too soon, for the horse flung his head around savagely and bared his teeth. But these teeth never met in Teddy's flesh, for at the same instant the boy sawed fiercely on the reins, jerking the head straight again.

Now the bronco settled down to the business on hand, and showed the two breathless watchers some of the finer points of bucking. But Teddy stuck, and not once did he "go to leather," as gripping the pommel of the saddle is called. At the end of several minutes, each of which seemed an eternity, the pony stopped as suddenly as he began, cocked one eye at the top rail of the corral fence, and sprang again into action, this time on a dead run.

"Watch it!" Roy yelled. "He'll never make it, Teddy! Pull him up! Pull him up!"

But Teddy had a look in his eyes not unlike the fire that gleamed in the eyes of the bronco. He was doing no "pulling up."

"Yeo-o-o-ow!" he shouted. "Go to it! We're off! Baby, if you clear that —"

There was no time for more. The horse had reached the rails. Teddy felt the muscles of his mount contract like steel springs, and then he was flying through the air, up, up, up —

"He's over!"

"Man, what a jump!"

The hind feet of the horse had just grazed the top bar. And now he stood outside the corral, trembling violently, but, somehow, appearing as if in making the tremendous leap he had proved himself and would henceforth be content with this. In other words, it seemed as though he had changed in a second from a "bad actor" to a real saddle horse.

Teddy gently rubbed the sides of the sweating animal.

"All right now, old boy?" he asked. "No more fireworks? Guess he'll do, Nick. Some one must have been feeding him on yeast. That was some jump!"

"I'll tell a maverick it was!" Roy was hurrying toward his brother. "Boy, you're lucky! I never thought he'd make it. And with that extra bar dad put up! That bronc is a *jumper*. What do you say, Nick?"

"Sure is!" Nick approached, and gazed at the horse closely. "Salivate me if he ain't as gentle-eyed as a rabbit! Teddy, you cured him. Didn't think it could be done. If I know anything about horses, that one'll make a fine ridin' pony."

Teddy climbed off, stiff legged.

"He put on quite a show for a while, didn't he? All right, Nick, let down the bars an' we'll bring him in again. I'll have another look at him to-morrow. Want to make sure he's broken."

A little later the boys were saddling their own mounts, Flash and Star. The new pony was standing calmly within the corral, and Teddy grinned at him.

"Dad ought to be back soon," Roy remarked, and he slid the bit gently into Star's mouth.

"Wish we'd gone along with him," came from Teddy. "Say, we could ride part of the way to meet him. How about it?"

"Sure," and Roy grinned. "The 8 X 8 is on the way to Hawley, isn't it? Yea, let's start to meet him. But if we reach Pete Ball's place, we won't stop in. Oh, no!"

"Chuck it," Teddy replied. "You know you're anxious to see Nell. Come on, let's be on our way."

CHAPTER VI

BAD NEWS

Teddy treated the riding of the wild bronco as an incident in the day's work. It might well have turned out disastrously for him, but, now that it was over, the youth thought no more about it except to remember that it would be well to ride him again to-morrow before the pony forgot his lesson. Thus, while the two boys rode toward Hawley, their conversation was mostly taken up with the note Mr. Manley had received and the possibility of trouble.

"Though I don't see exactly what they could do," Roy mused, shifting in his saddle.

The day was warm, even for Indian summer, the heat seemed to beat up from the stretch of bare ground the boys were riding over.

"I can't understand it!" exclaimed Teddy. "Those hombres are in jail, aren't they? What in thunder can they do? Unless they have a gang of friends around. And that isn't so likely. Honestly, I don't believe that Gilly Froud has a friend in the world. Why, even the men he rustled with, hate him. I guess we can count him out, anyway."

Roy removed his sombrero and ran his finger around the sweat band, bringing it forth as wet as though he had dipped it in a pail of water.

"I'm not worrying about Froud," he stated, picking up his reins, which he had allowed to fall loosely on Star's neck. "He's had his turn and has said his little piece. He won't do any more talking in public for a long time. But I tell you, Teddy, that puncher with the riding slouch has got me thinking. How about it — was he one of the rustlers?"

"Question — who struck Bill Patterson?" Teddy grinned. "That reminds me. Mother said that Curly — "

"Leaping lizards!" Roy groaned. "Can't you be serious for a minute? This is important, I tell you! Suppose the rustlers — er — well, suppose they — "

"No! They *coldn' t* do that! You know they couldn't! That 'ud be fearful — simply fearful! And, besides, I think it's going to rain to-morrow. No rustler wants to go out in the rain. 'Cause why? 'Cause somebody has to tell them to come in, and if there's no one around, they just get al-l-l-l wet."

"And there's another thing," Roy went on, ignoring his brother's somewhat sarcastic levity. "What or who is 'Reltsur?' I mean the name that was signed to the note."

"I know!" Teddy's face was alight with a sudden idea. "There's a fellow down at Eagles who just came to town. Gus Tripp was telling me about him — said he saw him when he rode in for the mail yesterday. Well, this geezer — "

"What about him?" Roy asked eagerly.

"He sells patent medicine! And I bet Reltsur is the name of one of his cures. Good for man or beast — positive cure or your money back. Read our testimonials. Mr. L. J. McPhoff, of Chickawalla, says: 'I have used Reltsur now for thirteen years. When I started I was only twenty years old. Now, I'm thirty-three.' Or hear what Mr. Specknoodle reports: 'I highly recommend Reltsur for — ' Hey, cut it out! Don't get that hat dirty!"

But it was too late. Roy had scaled his brother's sombrero as far as he could. Then he clucked to Star, and, yelling like an Indian, bore down upon the hat.

"Pony express!" he yelled. "Buck Wallace in his famous picture 'The Bad man of the Bad Lands!' You! Yip-yip-e-e-e-e!"

Leaning over, he swept the hat from the ground as he dashed by. Then he wheeled, and, with a bow, presented it to Teddy.

"Just found it," he said, with a grin. "Yours, maybe? Allow me! Rather warm isn't it? But it'll be cooler this winter, I expect."

"My nice new Stetson," Teddy remarked ruefully as he dusted it off. "Suppose Star had stepped on it? Fine pony express you are!"

"He didn't," Roy said, with a laugh. "Now what was that about Curly, Teddy?"

"Well, who do *you* think Reltsur is?"

Roy let out a roar of laughter. Then for some minutes Teddy was content to discuss their visitor of the night, but neither of the boys reached any conclusion, and at last they dismissed the subject.

Both were eager to hear what their father had to report when he returned from Hawley. The trail they were on led to the town where the rustlers were jailed, and the boys had hopes of meeting Mr. Manley on his way home. Yet the 8 X 8 Ranch was not out of their way, and if they missed their father, Teddy and Roy would not be at all averse to stopping off for a short visit.

The 8 X 8 was owned by Peter Ball, a neighbor and friend of Bardwell Manley. His two nieces from New York were paying their first visit to the West, and, as Teddy had said, they were planning to stay all winter at the Ball ranch. Since the girls were young and comely, it is not to be wondered at that Teddy and Roy took advantage of every opportunity to see them. Ethel Carew, or "Curly," as the boys called her, seemed to hold special attraction for Teddy, while Nell Willis and Roy found each other's company mutually agreeable.

Thus, while both boys declared their purpose in riding out was to meet Mr. Manley, they would not bother to avoid the 8 X 8 by circuitous riding.

After his imitation of the "pony express," Roy settled into a moody silence, which all Teddy's efforts failed to disperse. Roy was given to these spells of thoughtfulness, though perhaps more so lately than before. His brother had accused him of being in love, but Roy denied this so calmly that Teddy knew that the thrust was ineffectual. The only other conclusion was that the older youth felt a responsibility growing with his years, and was taking more of a burden upon his shoulders than the occasion warranted.

As they rode along, Teddy stole a glance at the boy at his side. He noted the stiffness of the back, and the firm set of the head upon the shoulders.

"He's worrying about something," the younger lad thought. "He always takes everything so seriously! I'll bet it's that note. Maybe I shouldn't have kidded him about it. But, golly, there's no reason to get so low over it! Roy!" he said aloud. "Snap out of it! What's on your mind?"

"Who, me?" the other turned, startled. Then he grinned. "Was I asleep? Guess I must have been thinking. What was that you asked me?"

"Why, I just wanted to know what you were mooning about. You were riding along staring straight ahead as though you were in a trance. What in thunder is the matter with you lately, Roy?"

"Oh, nothing," the boy answered, laughing a bit uneasily. "I was wondering about that note, that's all. I'd hate to have anything happen just when we've got over our trouble with the rustlers. Although I'll admit we had some exciting times for a while," and Roy's eyes sparkled. Then he grew grave again. "But dad sort of counts on us to keep things going, you know. That's why I'm anxious to see what he has to say when he gets back from Hawley. That gang can — "

"Aw, what can they do?" Teddy demanded. "They're all in jail. Forget about 'em, Roy. What's the use of crossing bridges before you reach 'em?"

"That's true enough. But you know I saw that slouched puncher right after the landslide. If he's really one of the rustlers, he doesn't bear us any love, I reckon." The boy patted Star on the side to brush off a fly. "And seeing him right after the landslide — "

"Well, for Pete's sake!" Teddy burst out, "you don't think he started the slide, do you? Roy, come to life! Be yourself! Now how in the name of cackling cows could he have anything to do with that?"

Roy shook his head.

"I don't mean that," he explained. "But it sure looked as though he'd been following us. At least it did to me. How'd he know when to ride by last night? He timed that perfectly! By jinks, I'll bet he was watching us all the time!"

"Maybe," Teddy said laconically. "But wondering won't get us any place. We'll have to sit tight and watch our step, that's all. Come on, it's gettin' late."

As they rode forward at a faster gait, Teddy suddenly called his brother's attention to a figure on horseback coming toward them.

"It's dad!" Roy exclaimed. Then, as the figure neared: "He looks worried, too. Wonder what happened?"

"Howdy, boys!" called Mr. Manley, as he rode up. "Come to meet the old man, hey?"

"What's the news, Dad?" Teddy asked eagerly.

A frown came to Mr. Manley's face.

"Not so good," he said slowly. "We won't be able to prosecute those hoss thieves after all."

Hesitating, he drew a corncob pipe from his pocket and stuck it between his lips, unlighted.

"The whole caboodle of 'em escaped yesterday," he added tersely.

"Escaped? The prisoners?" Roy Manley looked at his father incredulously. "What do you mean, Dad?"

"Just what I said, son," and the pipe never wavered between the set teeth. "They took French leave. Yesterday morning, early — 'bout five o'clock, they said — two men started to shoot up the town. Of course the sheriff an' his two deputies got on the job. When they come back, after chasin' the gunman out, they found the jail empty an' the bars in the windows sprung. Guess that's all."

CHAPTER VII

A FLIVVER MESSENGER

Teddy and Roy looked at each other with startled eyes. That rider on Mica Mountain, the puncher who sat slouched in the saddle!

"Any trace of 'em?" Teddy asked.

"Not any, son. They vamoosed clean. But lemme tell you something funny. Two days ago they decided the jail was too crowded an' they moved Froud over to the calaboose in Marxsted. An' he's the only one of the rustlers they still got! Can you beat that? So, at all events, Gilly Froud is where he won't do any harm. Anything new at the ranch?"

The ride back home was occupied with a discussion of the situation. Teddy and Roy had, of course, given up the idea of riding on to the 8 X 8, as they were anxious to know their father's plan of action. Yet, as Teddy suggested, what could they do? It would be useless to go after the escaped rustlers. Besides, there was no need for it. Until the enemy showed his hand, they just had to sit tight. Of course it would be well to have some extra men ride herd, but, somehow, both Mr. Manley and the two boys felt the blow, if it did fall, would come from another direction.

"Maybe we're makin' a mountain out of a molehill," Mr. Manley declared, as he stood near the hitching rail by the corral, the horses having been watered. "Those hoss thieves are loose. What more do they want? Why should they bother us? If they want to start up another gang and go back to rustling again, that's up to them. But I have a hunch that's not what they're after. They've had their fill of that game. And, besides, the sheriff said that two of those babies came from New York. That mean anything? Remember the barkeeper in Rimor's place who tried to crash me with a bottle when I went in after that hombre with the checkered shirt?"

"Sure do!" Teddy remarked excitedly. "He came from New York, too, didn't he? They must be importing a bunch of gunmen down here! Do you think the bird in Rimor's is one of the gang, Dad?"

"Wouldn't surprise me a bit," Mr. Manley answered. "He's not there any more, you know. He ducked out. It may be — I don't say it is — but it's just possible that he and his friends got the rustlers out of jail. Boys, I hate to say it, but somehow it looks like trouble was stirrin' up."

"But why?" Teddy asked insistently. "What makes you say that, Dad? Roy's been like that all day, too. Why the worry?"

"So you been thinkin' too, have you, Roy?" the ranch owner repeated, glancing over at his son. "Well, I'll tell you, Teddy. All of us have our friends and our enemies. When my dad — your grandfather, that was — first settled here there was nothin' but a lot of space. Pop Burns can tell you about that. Then later Eagles came, and with it some punchers that wanted money without workin' for it. About six years ago they wanted me to go into a scheme of weighting the cattle scales down at the railroad corral. But I soon set 'em right on that!"

Teddy and Roy nodded.

"Pop told us," Roy stated. "That put you sort of in wrong, didn't it?"

"Yep. Then a queer gang from the East began to head for Eagles. You know most of 'em I guess. That barkeeper was the worst of the lot. They joined up with the element that had it in for me. You know the result — how we had our horses stolen and our cattle rustled. Then, when we landed the gang an' jailed 'em, I figured they were out of the way for a while. But now — they're out. An' I get this note."

Slowly he took the paper from his pocket and gazed at it.

"Reltsur," he mused. "Sounds like a foreign name. Well, by jinks, whoever he is — " The man's eyes blazed and he crumpled the paper up and flung it savagely from him. "Whoever he is, if he fools around here he'll wish he hadn't! An' that's that!"

Turning, he strode into the house.

"You were right, Roy," Teddy remarked in a low voice, watching his father's form pass through the door. "Dad does take it seriously. He's all het up. I wonder what — Oh, fishcakes! What's the use of wondering? I'm going in."

The next morning when Mr. Manley came toward the bunk-house to speak to one of the punchers, Nick, who was standing in the doorway, noticed with surprise that the boss had a six-gun fastened to his belt.

"Goin' huntin', boss?" the puncher asked.

"Mebbe," Mr. Manley answered laconically. "Want to be ready in case any two-legged rattlesnakes are wanderin' around. Where's Jim Casey?"

"Around back. Want him?"

"Yea."

When Jim approached he was given directions to set three more men to riding the cattle.

"Tell Teddy who they'll be," Mr. Manley directed. "He's foreman this week. If you want anything else, ask him. And listen. If you see any strangers around here, ask 'em their business. Especially if you see a puncher that rides leanin' a little to the left in his saddle. I guess you all know who I mean. I'm going to head for town. Be back in a few hours."

"The boss means business," Gus Tripp declared, when Mr. Manley had left. "There's Teddy. Yo-o-o, Teddy! Yore dad was just here. Told Jim to put some extra riders out."

"I know," Teddy nodded. "Who do you want, Jim? How about Rad Sell, Nat Raymond, and — well, you want to take it, Gus?"

"Sure," Gus answered. "Nick can hang around here. But don't you go serenadin' Norine, Nick. Guess I'd better have Pop keep an eye on you."

"Dry up!" Nick growled. "You'll have your hands full without worryin' about Norine."

At that moment Roy came from the ranch house and walked toward the group.

"Dad around?" he asked.

"Just left," Teddy replied. "Went to Eagles, didn't he, Nick? Say, did he have a gun on?"

"He did," Gus drawled. "Said he might meet up with some two-legged rattlers. Yore dad worried about that note, Roy?"

"He's sore about it, at any rate," Roy answered. "Dad doesn't like any one to try to bluff him. Then, too, he's kind of waiting for something to start, I think. You knew the horse thieves that we rounded up are loose again?"

"Yep. All our work for nothin'! Well, let 'em try some more rustlin', that's all I ask. *This* time we'll salivate 'em."

"Dad said they might try another game," Teddy declared. "He didn't say what, but he mentioned the fact that there are several gunmen from the East mixed up in the crowd. Can't tell what that bunch'll pull. You men that are riding cattle, don't stay in one place too long. Keep moving, and try to ride fence as much as you can. If you see a break that looks suspicious, report it. We can't afford to take chances, because there's a big shipment of Durhams due to go out this month, you know. For the love of Pete! Look who's coming!"

Down the road swept a cloud of dust, punctuated by the sound of a horn, and now and then a hoarse shout. The cloud drew up by the bunkhouse, and slowly drifted away to disclose a flivver, with a freckled, grinning youth at the wheel.

"Howdy!" this dusty apparition exclaimed. "It's me. Me an' my little peanut roaster. Waddaya say?"

"Hello, Bug Eye!" Teddy cried. "What's the news? Why the rush?"

"Rush!" Bug Eye looked at the speaker reproachfully. "I wasn't rushin'. I was goin' slow! You want to see me when I'm in a hurry! Er — oh, yea, I knew I came over here fer somethin'. I got a message fer Belle."

Bug Eye was a hand on the 8 X 8, and Mr. Ball frequently made use of him to drive one of the ranch cars. Bug Eye was always delighted to oblige, and had almost forsaken horses for the "puddle jumper."

Now he reached laboriously inside an upper pocket of his shirt and un-earthed tobacco, "makin's," and finally a soiled envelope.

"She's a little dirty," he apologized, "but I guess she ain't hurt none. Got that way from Lizzie hoppin' around so much. Baby, this here tin mule is a flyin' fool! One minute she's on the road an' the next she's skimmin' over a cloud, or — or somethin'. Want a ride? Take you any place! I just put in a new dofunny, an she goes like a jack-rabbit. How about it, Teddy? Roy? Take a little jaunt? She's good. Bust her hide, she's good! Why, on the way over I seen a prairie dog that was goin' the same way I was, an' —
"

"Save it, save it!" Nick yelled. "Why don't you write a book, Bug Eye? Snakes! I never see a man that could talk as much as you an' say so little."

"Yes?" Bug Eye glanced at Nick calmly. "Maybe you don't understand. You know I talk English, an' I guess it's kind of hard for you birds to catch on. Here's the note, Roy. Fer yore sister. Got anything to eat in there, Gus? Where's Sing Lung? He ought to have some beans warmin'.'"

Roy took the missive from Bug Eye, and the messenger stretched high and entered the bunk-house, carefully oblivious of Nick's taunting reply. The note was addressed to "Miss Belle Ada Manley," and, boylike, Roy held it to his nose and inhaled deeply.

"Perfume?" Teddy asked, grinning.

"Tobacco," Roy answered briefly, making a wry face. "It was buried in Bug Eye's pocket. Let's take it in to Belle."

Within the ranch house, the two boys stood about in careless attitudes as their sister ripped open the envelope. Belle paused and looked up.

"Something?" she questioned innocently.

"Come on, Belle — have a heart," Teddy murmured. "What's in it?"

"Oh, this!" The girl looked at the note calmly. Slowly she read it through, and then folded it carefully and replaced it in the envelope.

"Well?" Roy burst out.

"Oh, you want to know what she says?" Belle asked. "Why, it's — it's just a note."

"Yea? What's it say?"

"Why, Nell and Ethel want me to — is that mother calling?"

"No! Go on!"

"They want me to visit them. That's all."

"So that's all?"

The two boys turned away.

"Well, they want to be remembered to you two. And they want you to stay to dinner to-morrow night when you take me over."

"Oh, they do! Why didn't you say so?"

36

"I forgot."

"All right!" Teddy and Roy glared in mock anger. "We'll remember this!" Then in chorus, "Re-e-e-e-venge!"

And they stalked out of the room, to execute a war dance in the hall.

CHAPTER VIII

A GREAT FEAR

The incident of the escaped rustlers was forgotten for the time while Belle prepared for her visit to the 8 X 8. Mr. Manley discarded his gun the day she was to leave, whether because of what he had heard at Eagles or because he deemed it no longer necessary, was a matter for speculation. At all events, he had recovered his good humor and directed many quips at the care Roy and Teddy were taking with their appearance before they set out. It had been arranged that the brothers were to drive Belle over in a car and return later in the evening.

"I see you boys are goin' some place," Mr. Manley said, as he stood at the door of their room, hands deep in his pockets, corncob pipe emitting clouds of fragrant smoke.

"Taking a ride," Teddy answered, without turning. He was adjusting his tie at the mirror. Roy, beside him, was occupied in the same manner. Teddy just touched his brother with his elbow, and winked in the glass.

"Well — er — any particular place?" their father asked innocently.

"Vienna," Teddy replied, grinning.

"Vienna, hey?" Mr. Manley considered this for a moment. "Goin' to a show there?"

"Nope," and Teddy winked again. "Just going to loaf around a bit."

"Goin' to loaf around — " Then Mr. Manley woke up and sent out a roar of laughter. "Good shot, Teddy! You're gettin' better! Be almost a match for me soon. Well, good luck to you, an' don't take any wooden nickels!" Still chuckling, he tramped away.

"Dad seems to be O. K. now," Roy remarked, as he gave his tie a final twist. "I'm glad to notice it. I don't like to see him worried. Come along, you look beautiful! Get a move on! We've got to get started."

"Just a second."

Opening the top drawer of the dresser, Teddy took out two pistols, both smaller than the large guns usually carried in that vicinity. One of these he handed to Roy and the other he placed in an upper inside pocket under his left arm. Roy nodded in approval.

"Just in case," Teddy explained, and, putting on their coats, the two boys descended the stairs.

They told their father, out of hearing of Mrs. Manley, however, who might worry unnecessarily, that they were armed. The ranch owner commended their foresight and remarked that he was about to suggest it himself. He knew the boys were to be depended upon. Living on the range brings self-reliance early in life, and Mr. Manley felt proud of the fact that his sons were true men of the West — courageous and upright.

As the car rolled out of the ranch yard with Roy driving and Belle and Teddy beside him in the front seat, Sing Lung burst from the door of the cook-house.

"Late!" he yelled. "You late!"

"What's he mean — 'late?' " Teddy asked curiously.

"He means wait," Belle answered, with a smile. "Hold up for a minute, Roy. He wants to give us something."

Sing Lung ran towards them, a package in his hand. A broad grin lighted his face.

"You maybe get hungly, yes?" he said, placing the package in Belle's lap. "I flix lunch!"

"That's very kind of you, Sing Lung," Belle declared, smiling her gratitude. Belle was plainly the cook's favorite. "We'll be glad to have this. Thank you, a lot!"

"All lite!" with a still wider grin. "You wal-com'. Goo'-bye. Have nice time! Jumpee allee slidewalks!"

"He means skip the gutter," Teddy explained, laughing, as the car proceeded. "Nick must have taught him that. 'Jump the slidewalks!' That's a hot one! Trust the Chinks to get everything backwards."

"Never mind; Sing Lung is one good Chink," Roy declared. "This lunch will sure come in handy."

" 'Jump the slidewalks' means 'skip the gutter,' and 'skip the gutter' means — perhaps, 'jump the slidewalks?' Now, just what did Sing Lung mean, boys?"

But Belle's brothers refused to be drawn into explanations or argument.

Seven miles out from their home ranch a report suddenly sounded from under the car, and it lurched crazily. Roy jammed on the brakes vigorously.

"Blowout," he said shortly. "Might have known that 'ud happen! Just when we get rolling along nicely, the tire goes. Well," he jumped from the car and bent down, "she's done for, all right. And any one who pulls that old chestnut about 'only flat on one side' will have to fix it all alone! Come on Teddy — you posing for a statue?"

Teddy grinned, and alighted, as did Belle. Luckily, there were two good spares on the rear, so there was no danger of a long delay. The jack was soon out, and one of the tires taken from the rack.

When Roy had lifted the spare in position for tightening the lugs, he stood back for a moment and looked around him.

"This is a great place for a rattler," he declared, wiping the sweat from his brow. "Pop said he saw a whole nest of 'em somewhere around here."

"Thought you said Pop was full of crazy ideas?" Teddy retorted, thinking of the porcupine incident when he had told Roy about Pop's believing the "shooting quill" theory.

"Well, he may not know porcupines, but he sure does know about snakes," the elder youth asserted. "And if you're wise, you won't go fooling around a spot where Pop says there are rattlers. This is one swell day for 'em, too! Hand me that lug wrench, will you, Teddy?"

Teddy complied, and assisted Roy in fastening the tire to the rim. When it was firmly attached, Roy straightened and heaved a sigh of relief. As he did so his eyes swept the horizon, and he stared intently, one hand shading his eyes.

"What is it, Roy?" Belle asked, looking at her brother.

"Dust," Roy answered. "See it, Teddy? Top of that hill. Whoever's making it must be just below the rise. Wonder if it's some of Pete Ball's men? Likely to be. Come on, let's get this stuff away and start. We haven't got far to go, but that sun's hotter than all get out. Teddy, how about making yourself useful, and putting some of these tools away?"

"Sure," his brother answered. "Thought you wanted to do it all yourself."

A pair of pliers had fallen to the ground from the running board, and Teddy stooped to pick them up, his other hand resting on the door of the car, while he groped for the tool, bending down low.

"Golly, it's sure hot!" he exclaimed, still groping and searching. "Why couldn't the tire have blown out under a tree? Say, where in thunder are those pliers, anyhow?"

"Maybe it 'ud help if you *looked* for 'em, instead of watching that cloud of dust," Roy declared, grinning. "Belle, can't you help your little brother find the pliers?"

"Got 'em!" Teddy suddenly exclaimed, as his hand closed over them. "They were away under the car, and I couldn't see gettin' down in this dirt to look for 'em. Anyway —"

He started to withdraw his hand. There was a sudden loud "whir-r-r" as though a strip of tin were rapidly bent and released. Roy saw Teddy's whole body give a convulsive shudder and watched his face go deathly pale. Pop Burns' warning flashed to his mind.

"Teddy!" he cried, jumping forward. "Your hand!"

Belle screamed, and ran to her brother's side. Quickly she seized the left arm that had been under the auto and turned it over so that the back of the hand was uppermost. A thin line of blood showed red against the tan.

Teddy looked at it as though he were examining a curiosity. Then he laughed — at least, that is the only word to describe the sound that came from his lips. In a moment he stopped, and caught his breath.

"Got me," he said simply.

The three stood by the side of the car, shocked into silence. Belle retained her hold on Teddy's arm. Roy, his eyes wide, stared at the few drops of blood. Teddy's shoulders were thrown back, every muscle rigid. He looked straight ahead.

Roy was the first to move. He reached out quickly, and seized his brother's wrist in a firm grip, squeezing it with all his strength.

"Belle," he said in a low voice, "reach into my pocket and bring out a handkerchief. We've got to make a tourniquet, so the poison won't get up his arm. Quick!"

Drawing in a deep breath, Belle obeyed. Teddy swayed slightly, then got a grip on himself. His teeth clenched.

"Roy," he said quietly, "hold my arm over a way."

Wondering, Roy changed his position. Teddy reached inside his coat with his right hand, and drew out a gun. Then Roy understood.

Whatever happened, they must kill that rattler. He had bitten — he must die. His head must be blown from his body, and they must cut him with lead until his lashings ceased and the tail grew still.

Eyes blazing, Teddy once more bent over. Roy retained his desperate grip on his brother's wrist. Belle, eyes wide with horror, stepped back. The scene was almost too much for her, Western bred though she was. Teddy, bitten by a crawling death, calmly intent on just one thing — killing the snake that had bitten him! Roy holding back the poison from his brother's body with one hand, while he steadied him with the other, so that he might not miss!

With her heart in her throat, Belle waited for the shot. After the snake had been killed — what? She could picture Teddy sitting stoically in the car as it careened its way toward the ranch — Teddy, his arm black from the tourniquet, perhaps remarking that Roy would have to take charge of the place for the rest of the week and would he see that Flash got enough exercise, and all the while his lips were twisted with burning pain! Teddy!

Would he never fire? What was he waiting for?

"Shoot! Oh, shoot!" Belle gasped. "Teddy — kill him and come away!"

Still the two boys were bent over, staring beneath the car. Then Belle saw Roy slowly release his hold on his brother's wrist. A sound strangely like a chuckle came from him. What — what had happened?

"Teddy! Roy!" Belle cried. "What is it? Why are you waiting? The snake — "

For a moment she thought her brothers had gone mad, and well she might, for, straightening up, the boys burst into roars of laughter. They leaned weakly against the side of the car, Teddy's gun hanging limply, his body shaking with mirth! Roy was pounding him on the back, while he himself was scarcely able to stand. This was more than laughter, it was almost hysteria — the hysteria of great and sudden relief.

Then when Roy caught sight of his sister's face, he sobered.

"It's all right, sis," he declared, tears of laughter still in his eyes. "Don't look so scared. We're not crazy — and Teddy isn't hurt. He didn't get bitten by a rattler at all!"

"Didn't — didn't — get bitten! Roy, I don't understand — "

"Look!"

He motioned to his sister to bend down and peer under the car. As he did so Roy's hand reached out — and there followed that same "whir-r-r-r" they had heard before.

"Get it?" Roy exclaimed, his laughter starting up again. "This — this piece of tin under the running board! See? When I hit it, it whirs. Teddy's hand scraped it, and it buzzed and scratched his hand. And we thought it was a rattler! Oh, baby, what a couple of saps! Wait till dad and Nick hear about this!"

"He didn't get bitten?" Belle repeated, hardly able to realize what had happened. "There wasn't any snake?" she questioned incredulously.

"Nary snake — just this tin! That's all!"

With a sob of relief, Belle threw her arms around her brother's neck.

"Oh, Teddy!" she gasped. "I'm so glad — so glad! Oh, Teddy, I thought you were going to die! And when you were bending over with the gun, just thinking about killing the old rattlesnake, I — I — "

"Hey, sis, come out of it!" Teddy said a trifle shakily. He kissed her full on the lips. "Thought you'd have to play jokes on Roy all alone after this, did you? Well, I'm still here — and we won't forget how he teased you the other night on the porch, either! We'll get him for that! I got a great idea — only he's listening now. When we get home — "

It was just this that was needed to calm Belle. The strain she had been under had been terrific, and it is no wonder that, when it was over, she broke down. But now she dried her eyes and raised her head.

"Only a piece of tin!" she exclaimed, a smile coming over her face. "And even Teddy thought he had been bitten! But whatever it was — I'm glad you're all right, Teddy dear! And now, I have an idea."

Belle was once more herself. Patting her hair, she walked steadily toward the car. Then she flung open the door and held up a white package. It was the lunch Sing Lung had prepared.

"Gentlemen," she cried, "dinner is served! Long live Sing Lung! Come and get it!"

CHAPTER IX

ROY'S SUSPICIONS

As the Manley boys and their sister sat in the car munching sandwiches, now and then Teddy would glance at his hand, which still showed the red scratch, and shake his head in wonder that such a strange mistake could have happened. It hardly seemed possible that one could imagine he had been bitten by a rattler when there was no snake within miles, for all they knew. Yet, the "whir-r-r" of that tin certainly did sound like the warning of a side-winder. And when his hand had been injured at the same time — what other conclusion could be drawn?

Of course both Roy and Teddy knew that a snake's bite would usually be nothing more than two small punctures in the flesh, yet if the hand was being withdrawn when the fangs hit it, the flesh could easily be torn.

The two boys and their sister did not talk much of Teddy's experience. Somehow, it hardly seemed the thing to joke about, even though it had turned out so fortunately. The laughter of the boys on discovering the piece of tin was not born of true mirth, but was a natural outlet for the strain they had been under.

It took some time for the travelers to recover their usual spirits, but Sing Lung's food helped a great deal, and when the sandwiches were finished they set off once more toward the 8 X 8 with lighter hearts. And as they proceeded, the reaction set in — a reaction of happy, carefree joyousness. The boys thought of Nell and Curly, and, as always happens after a period of depression, anticipation of coming pleasure swelled to mountainous proportions in their minds. The whole world suddenly appeared rose-colored, and the most prosaic things in it took on a carnival aspect. The sun-drenched trees they passed seemed to smile at them. It was no longer hot, but only pleasantly warm — a wonderful day for anything.

"Yay, look at ole cottontail" Teddy yelled, pointing ahead. "Go get him, Roy! Step on it!"

"Ri-i-i-ight!" sang out Roy, and pressed the accelerator. The car shot forward, Belle mingling her laughter with that of her brothers.

"Ten dollars if you keep that cab in sight!" she called, melodramatically pointing to the rabbit scurrying ahead. "And another ten if you catch it before it reaches the ship! Don't spare the horses!"

"Yes, ma'am!" came the answer. "I suppose Miss Vere De Vere is in it with her uncle, who is kidnapping her so that he can get control of the family fortune — the dir-r-r-rty rat!"

"And then some!" Belle laughed, her eyes sparkling. "Roy, you ought to be on the stage. Say, you'd better slow down before you get another blowout."

Her brother saw the wisdom of this advice, and took on a slower pace while the rabbit disappeared in the brush. The high spirits of the three were by no means lessened when they reached the 8 X 8, and they piled out with loud yells. Nell and Ethel ran into the yard when they heard the uproar.

"The stage has arrived!" Teddy shouted, grinning. "Good morning, Ethel and Nell. I hope our visit finds you well. It is with great pleasure we see you again — and — and — Now what else did mother tell me to say?"

"Dry up, Teddy," Roy laughed, walking toward the two girls. "Don't mind him. He gets that way every once in a while, but he's harmless. How are you, Nell and Ethel? We brought our little sister over to see you."

"Little!" Belle laughed scornfully. "I'm almost as big as you are, Roy Manley! And I can shoot almost as well as you can, too! Oh, Nell, what a lovely dress! Where *did* you get it!"

After Belle and the two boys had removed some of the stains of travel, they all gathered in the dining room for lunch. Belle said that they had had some sandwiches on the way, but Teddy quickly explained that they were *very small*, and, anyway, one couldn't live on sandwiches. And, with this excuse for the coming slaughter, he and Roy proceeded to "go to work" on the very excellent food before them.

In the afternoon, while the girls were resting, the two boys wandered over toward the bunk-house to talk to Bug Eye, who was detailed to make out a list of the things needed on the ranch before the fall round-up. He was busily engaged when the brothers entered, and paused with his pencil to the paper and looked up.

"Say," he began, "is 'saddle' spelt 'a-l' or 'e-l'?"

"The 'X' is silent, like in fish," Teddy replied. "What are you doing, Bug Eye? Writing notes to the cows?"

"Not any," came from the puncher, as he stretched and yawned widely. "The boss has got me to figerin' out how much stuff we lost durin' the summer an' how much we need. Some job! Rather be punchin' dogies any day. Say, what you boys been doin' with yoreselves? Hear any more about that gang from Hawley? Nick Looker told me about the note you got."

Roy flung one leg over the table Bug Eye was writing on, and glanced idly at the piece of paper scribbed over with figures.

"The jail in Hawley was cleaned out," he said slowly. "You knew about that?"

"No! You don't say!" Surprise was written on Bug Eye's face. "You mean to tell me them rustlers are loose again, after all the trouble we had to round 'em up? Great snakes! How'd that happen, an' when?"

"The other day," Teddy answered, watching his brother closely. Roy seemed intent on the paper spread on the table before him. "The sheriff and his deputies were chasing some would-be gunmen out of town, and when they came back the prisoners were gone. Probably away on a week-end visit."

"Now, what do you know about that?" Bug Eye shook his head. "Froud, too? He gone?"

"Not quite," Teddy replied, and told of Froud's removal to another jail before the delivery. "So he's still sittin' out of the sun!"

"Say, Bug Eye!" Roy exclaimed suddenly, "you got that wrong." He pointed to the paper. "That should be a capital R. If Mr. Ball is going to see this paper, you might as well have it right. See? Make that a capital."

"Shore," Bug Eye replied, and laboriously effected the correction. Roy watched him carefully. "Thanks, Roy. Guess that kind of slipped by me. How long you boys goin' to stay with us?"

Teddy answered, and the conversation came to a close when Roy suggested that they were interrupting the puncher's work. The two boys wandered back toward the ranch house. The moment they were out of hearing of Bug Eye, Teddy asked:

"Say, Roy, what was the big idea? You were watching that paper Bug Eye was writing on pretty closely. And rawhide doesn't start with a capital R. How come?"

"Just a little plan of my own," Roy replied vaguely. "That note, you know. Signed Reltsur. I thought maybe —"

"That Bug Eye wrote it?" Teddy inquired in an incredulous voice. "Well, for the love of Pete, what ever put that into your head? Bug Eye do a thing like that? Not on your life!"

"I know it now," Roy said shortly. "I don't know why I suspected him. Just one of those crazy ideas you get, I guess. That capital R seemed to stick in my mind. Come on, I think Belle and the two girls are around somewhere. Let's go and see."

Teddy shook his head slowly and followed his brother. What was getting into Roy? Thinking Bug Eye wrote that note! Why, Bug Eye didn't ride slouched in the saddle! He forked a bronc like any other puncher in those parts.

Then, a few days before, Roy had mentioned seeing the slouched rider directly after the landslide when he was searching for Teddy. As though the strange puncher could have had anything to do with that slide! Yes, Roy was sure acting queer lately. As far as Teddy could see, there was no reason for immediate worry. Even if the rustlers were out of jail and determined on revenge, they might be forestalled by guarding the cattle well. True, his father had declared he thought the thieves might try other tactics. But, after all, what could they do? Suppose they had some real gunmen in their crowd? They would scarcely take to shooting a man in the back as he rode along.

The note had said the charge against the rustlers must not be pressed. Well, they were out of jail now, and, as Mr. Manley had said, what more did they want? Why should they bother to avenge themselves on men who had only protected their own cattle? It didn't seem reasonable. Yet, Teddy thought, his father *was* worried. Perhaps he knew more than he had told. Teddy had never known his father to show worry unless there was good reason for it. If he went to town carrying a gun, a thing he had not done for years except the time he was actually running down the horse thieves, he must anticipate trouble of some sort.

Teddy shrugged his shoulders and gave up the problem.

The two boys found Nell and Ethel showing Belle some new flowers that had lately come up. As Teddy and Roy approached the girls turned.

"Want soma nice, fresh hunyons?" Ethel called out.

"Nope," Teddy returned, grinning. "Taka some strumberries, you got. What's this, a garden party?"

"Tour of investigation," Nell answered. "Oh, Roy, I want to show you these sunflowers! Aren't they beautiful?"

"I'll tell a maverick!" Roy answered, and, as Nell looked up, she saw that he was staring at her instead of at the sunflowers. She blushed, and bent quickly over to examine closely some wild roses.

The time passed pleasantly, and dinner was soon announced. Roy lingered at the door watching the sunset, which was especially brilliant tonight, until Teddy and Belle each took an arm and pulled him in.

"But just look at those colors!" he persisted. "Why, no artist could paint them! They look like — like flames from a forest fire."

"Sure," Teddy said, grinning at Ethel. "Or maybe like a ripe tomato smashed against a white wall. Come on in and eat, you old dreamer. I'm hungry. Then you can tell Nell how much the landslide looked like the volcano scene in the 'Fall of Pompeii.' "

Roy made a friendly pass at his brother, who ducked, and the two entered and seated themselves at the table, which was decorated with flowers in honor of their visit, and it was not long before the beauty of sunsets was forgotten in the enjoyment of rare roast beef, carrots, and mashed potatoes.

CHAPTER X

A MAN IN THE CORRAL

At nine o'clock that evening the boys started for home. Roy had half-heartedly suggested leaving earlier, but he was overruled. So it was not until the moon was well above the horizon that the two young ranchers got away. Belle was to stay at the 8 X 8 for a few days, after which Roy and Teddy were to come for her.

Good-byes were said, and the boys started. As the car rolled toward home, Teddy, who was driving, sang softly under his breath. Roy was content to sit quietly and observe the splendor of the prairie night.

The white moonlight painted the ground with an almost phosphorescent glow. On either side of the road quakermasts reared their heads, like tall, gaunt giants. Now and then would come the cry of some animal in the distance, weirdly human. The hills ahead seemed to be crouched in attitudes of slumber.

Teddy squirmed in his seat.

"Itch," he declared briefly, as Roy looked at him. "Flea, maybe."

"Good heavens!" Roy groaned. "On a night like this, you talk about itches and fleas! Man! where is your appreciation?"

"My what? Oh, my appreciation. Got it sewed up in my pocket, where I won't lose it. Say, Roy, you reckon that bunch that vamoosed from Hawley will really start something?"

"Hope not." A frown crossed the boy's face. "You know what a cattle war means in this country. Well, it seems to me those birds are laboring under the impression that they have something on us, and they think it's all right to injure dad if that will square their account with the X Bar X. Doesn't make any difference to them that they're outlaws. They figure the country owes them a living, I guess, and they'll take it by force if they can't get it for nothing."

There was silence for a few moments before Teddy said slowly:

"They're hanging around this section, and it's up to us to watch out. Forewarned is forearmed, you know. Golly! That moon is so bright I'll bet I could run without any glims. Look —" He switched off the headlights for a moment. The road stretched before him like a silvered path. Each rut and depression in it was clearly defined, so that Teddy had no trouble in guiding the car.

"Better turn 'em on again," Roy suggested, after a minute. "If the moon should slide under a cloud you'd be ditched in a second. I wonder —"

Just at that moment the very thing Roy had anticipated came to pass. The silvery glow was cut off as suddenly as a flashlight that is switched out. The wind, blowing at a fair rate of speed, had tossed a cloud between the prairie and the moon. Roy gave a yell.

"Jam on the brakes! Never mind the lights! Stop!"

Teddy obeyed, and with a screeching of brakebands the car came to a halt. Then Teddy threw the lights on once more. The front of the car was nearly off the road.

"Good thing the brakes held," Teddy remarked, grinning.

"I'll tell a maverick it is!" Roy retorted. "I suppose you just wanted to try 'em out, hey? After this you'd better leave the lights on, unless you want to haul this boiler out of a ditch."

"Yes, sir!" Teddy answered, with mock humility. "Anything you say, sir. We strive to please. Say —" He stopped and lowered his voice. "Listen! You hear anything?" He reached forward and turned off the ignition switch, killing the motor.

For a moment both boys sat in silence. The face of the moon was still clouded, so that darkness surrounded them. Then, in the distance, the boys heard the sound of a horseman — clickety-click, clickety-click, clickety-click —

"In a hurry," Roy said wonderingly. "Seems to be coming this way, too. Well —"

He hitched his left shoulder a trifle and brought his pistol forward. Teddy did the same.

"Shall we wait?" Teddy asked, glancing back and striving to pierce the blackness.

Roy shook his head.

"Let's not. If he wants us, he knows where to find us. Though the chances are it's only one of the men from the 8 X 8. Anyway, it's none of our business. Come along — step on it!"

Teddy started the motor again, and the car proceeded. As the moon lit the landscape with its beams once more, Roy turned and glanced back. But the road curved just here, and he could see no rider. Also, they could no longer hear the hoofbeats, which, if they were approaching, should have become louder.

"That's something else to worry about," Teddy said, with a grin. "Funny that we both took it for granted that whoever it was must be on *on* trail! We seem to be getting sillier every day. At least I do. Like this afternoon, when we had that snake scare."

"Forget it," Roy advised. "You were no worse than I was. I heard a noise — and I would have sworn it was a side-winder. So we're both in the same boat."

As they neared home, both boys were wondering about the rider they had heard from afar. Neither would admit this, afraid of being accused of nervousness, but, nevertheless, when they came in sight of the corral of the X Bar X, they glanced cautiously about the place before riding in.

Teddy made a complete circle of the ranch yard, looking keenly about. Roy did not remark on this strange behavior. As they neared the entrance to the yard for the second time, Roy stretched and yawned.

"Let's hit the hay," he suggested, letting his arms drop to his sides.

"Suits me," Teddy agreed. Then: "Kind of quiet here to-night; don't you think so, Roy?"

"What do you expect, a brass band?" his brother grinned. "Golly, Teddy, you don't mean to say it's getting you, too?"

"Is what getting me?" the other countered, though he knew well enough what Roy meant. He guided the car toward the garage. "What do you mean, Roy?"

"That note," his brother responded laconically. "And the horseman we heard — but didn't see. And the puncher who rides leaning to the left in the saddle. And the whole blamed, silly business! How about it — am I talking straight or shall I elucidate?"

Teddy climbed stiffly out of the driver's seat and walked toward the large doors of the auto shed. Halfway there he turned.

"I get you," the boy said shortly. "Roy, you're right. I've been thinking. These things that are happening, though they seem small and insignificant, all mean something. I'll lay a bet on that." He stopped and mused for a moment. "It's hard to explain, but I feel as though some one or something were waiting around to sock me in the neck with a juicy tomato when my back is turned. And I don't like it, by jinks! I don't like it! Why don't they start something? If the rustlers would show their hand, we'd know what we were up against. But this waiting, without knowing what for, is getting me sort of nervous, I don't mind saying!" He strode forward, and flung one of the doors shut savagely.

Roy was closing the other, and until the garage was closed and locked he did not speak.

"You're not the only one who feels that way," he then said in a low voice. "I've been thinking those things for the past two or three days. And let me tell you something — dad has too. He may not say much, but he's worried all the same. He hasn't quite gotten over the time we had with that bunch of horse thieves only a little while ago, and he doesn't want it to happen again. That's why he wanted more men to ride herd. When he went to Eagles a few days ago, he toted a gun. You knew that?"

Teddy grunted affirmatively. The two boys walked toward the house.

"He didn't have it on to-day, but maybe he took it off because he didn't want to worry mother," Roy went on. "Dad knows there are a few men in Eagles that wouldn't cry if he disappeared in a sort of general way, like being shot up. And he's not going to give them a gun, butt first — not if I know dad!"

Teddy nodded. He recalled the look on his father's face the other day in the yard, as, with a savage gesture, he had thrown the mysterious note to the ground.

"Dad certainly seems changed," Teddy said slowly. At the steps, leading to the porch of the house, the boys paused for a moment to take one last look around. From the corral came the noise of restless horses, moving about, rubbing against the bars, now and then neighing.

"Wonder what's bothering them," Roy said, more to himself than to Teddy. "I suppose it's just one of the nights when the cattle want to be walking around instead of resting. I notice that happens mostly on nights when the moon is full. Maybe that has something to do with it. Jimminy, it sounds like a horse convention going on. There — that's Star whinnying — I could tell him a mile off. I got a good notion to —"

"Come on, hit the hay," Teddy said, with a laugh. "You want to dream about rustlers all night? You will, by jinks, if you don't snap out of it. Star's all right. You don't have to sing him a lullaby every time he gets insomnia, you know. Let's go. Put the hall light out, will you?"

The young ranchers ascended the stairs softly to their room. In little more than five minutes both were ready for bed. Roy switched the light off and crawled under the covers.

Out in the corral the horses still moved restlessly. The figure of a man on foot, pressed against one of the far posts so as to be out of sight from the house, seemed to annoy the ponies greatly.

CHAPTER XI

NICK'S TRICK

A few days after the boys had taken Belle to the 8 X 8, Nick Looker, seated on the side of his bunk, was showing the assemblage a new trick he had lately acquired from a book called "A Hundred Ways to Amuse Your Friends."

About him were grouped several punchers of the X Bar X, and also Roy and Teddy. Nick held up his hand.

"Now the idea, gents, is this," he intoned. "I'm goin' to tear a dollar bill in ten pieces, then roll 'em up in this here handkerchief, and in a second — blooey! The dollar bill is whole an' entire and in as excellent a condition as before the demonstration — that means trick, Gus. Now watch me closely."

He reached in his pocket. The punchers leaned forward eagerly.

"What's the matter, Nick — forget how to do it?" Pop asked after a moment.

"Can't find a bill," Nick answered shortly. "Thought sure I had one. Any of you birds got a dollar he'll lend me for a minute?"

"What! To tear up?" Rad Sell demanded. "Not me! Think I'm crazy?"

"It's only a trick, you galoot!" Nick exclaimed disgustedly. "You'll get your bill back, don't worry about that. Think I want to keep it?"

"Wouldn't be surprised," Pop Burns said, in a matter-of-fact, calm voice. "I've known stranger things to happen."

Teddy nudged Roy, and they both grinned. This might prove interesting.

"Well, come on, come on!" Nick shouted impatiently. "If you guys want to see the trick — an' it's a mighty good one, too — you got to get me a bill. Come on, fork over! Don't be so tight! I won't hurt your old bill."

"Maybe none of 'em ain't got one, Nick," suggested Pop mildly. "Me, I ain't."

"Thought you said you was goin' to rip it in ten pieces?" came from Nat Raymond, in a curious tone. "How about that, Nick?"

"Sufferin' snakes, but you waddies are dumb! That's part of the trick — then I make the pieces come together again and the bill is as good as new! Hoppin' lizards, if I was as thick as you guys —"

"You have to have a one dollar bill?" Gus Tripp interrupted. "I got a ten here, but I sure hate to part with it. If anything should happen —"

"Nothin' will happen," Nick growled. "Sure, the ten is all right. Let's have it, Gus. I'll give it back in a minute."

Slowly Gus passed the bill over. With a sudden motion he brought it to his lips, and sighed deeply.

"Come back to yore papa," he murmured. "An' don't do no wanderin' around! Nick, take care of my baby!"

"This'll be good," Teddy whispered to his brother. "Look at Pop! He's sure interested."

Nick nonchalantly took the proffered bill. He looked at it carefully. Then he took a handkerchief from his pocket and held it up.

"This, ladies an' — I mean gents, is the handkerchief. An' here we have the bill, which I shall proceed to rip into ten pieces, each of equal length an' — an' something. I wish for you to examine both."

He passed the bill to Pop Burns and the cloth to Nat Raymond. "Look at 'em, boys, to see that there is no fake. Pop, note the serial numbers on to that there bill, so you will see that no substitution is to take place nowheres. Take yore time, gents, take yore time!"

"An' this is the bill yore goin' to rip?" Pop asked, turning it over in his hands.

"The every same bill."

"Let's see the handkerchief."

Nat passed it over.

"An' yore goin' to put the pieces of the bill in this here cloth an' make 'em come together again?"

"That's just what I'm a-goin' to do!"

Pop looked down at the bill again.

"An' yore goin' to rip this here bill in ten pieces, you say?"

"I am — each of equal length."

"This bill right here, hey?"

"That same bill!"

"Well —"

Pop held the ten dollar bill up to the light of one of the windows. Then, suddenly, he tore it squarely across the middle, and, before any one could stop him, he tore it again, and again, until all that remained of Gus's "baby" were ten green strips of paper, all of equal length. These Pop handed to Nick.

"There," he said with satisfaction. "They're all tore fer you. Let's see you do the trick." The veteran puncher's eyes were alight with anticipation.

Nick looked dully at the pieces of what was once a certificate entitling the holder to ten dollars in gold at the United States Treasury. He seemed stunned. One of the strips fell from the palm of his hand and floated slowly to the floor. Then Nick awoke.

"You crazy old coot!" he yelled. "You tore Gus's ten-spot all up! You ruined it! What was the idea, hey? What was the idea?"

"Ain't that what you wanted done?" Pop asked innocently, a frown of perplexity coming over his face. "You said you were goin' to tear it up, Nick — you know you did! Didn't he, fellers? You all heard him — didn't he say he was goin' to rip it up?"

"Yea, but *I* had to do it!" Nick raved. "Not you! Snakes, I can't do nothin' now! The bill's ripped, Gus! She's spoiled!"

"You mean to say you can't do the trick?" Gus asked incredulously, staring at the remains of his bill. "Roll 'em in the handkerchief, Nick, an' make 'em come together again! You got to! That's all the jack I got in the world an' pay-day a week off! Roll 'em up, Nick!"

"Jumpin' lizards, what good'll rollin' 'em do?" demanded Nick, a look of disgust on his face. "Course I can't do the trick now! Ask Pop to do it — maybe he knows how! He tore it up on you!"

"Me do it?" the veteran seemed mildly surprised. "Why, Nick, it's yore trick! I can't do no tricks! Go on, roll them pieces up an make 'em come out together. You can do it. Don't give up so soon."

"I tell you the trick is ruined!" Nick cried frantically. "I'm finished! I won't have nothin' more to do with it! I'm through!"

"Wait a second!" Gus stepped forward. "How about my ten-spot, Nick? Where's that? I gave it to you. Ain't you goin' to roll it up and give it back to me? Golly, Nick, you can take a crack at it anyhow, can't you? Maybe she'll work. You never know till you try. Go ahead, Nick — roll 'em up! I sure need that tenner!"

Nick threw his arms about wildly.

"Yore all cookoo! I can't do the trick now! Me, I had to rip the bill up, nobody else! That was part of the trick!"

"But what difference does it make who tore it?" Pop inquired anxiously. "She's tore, ain't she? That's what you wanted. An' here's the handkerchief. Put the pieces in it, Nick, an' say 'blooey', or whatever it is you say, to make 'em come together again. Then you can give the tenner back to Gus. You want to see the trick done, don't you, Gus?"

"I sure do!" was the positive answer.

Nick looked from one to the other in despair. On the faces of all but Pop and Gus were wide grins. This was something they hadn't counted on, and the boys were enjoying the situation to its full extent. Roy and Teddy were chuckling with glee.

Nick glanced down once more at the remnants of the bill. Slowly he shook his head.

"Guess it's on me," he said sadly. "Gus, I owe you ten. But by golly, it was Pop's fault! He ought to pay you, by rights. But I'll stick to my word.

I'll give you the tenner to-morrow, Gus." He reached out to take the hand-kerchief from Pop. He was too mad to suggest, or even think of, pasting the parts of the bill together.

"So you can't do it, hey?" the old rancher demanded.

"Nope! No can do. Here, take these for a souvenir, Pop. You deserve 'em." And Nick laughed bitterly as he dropped the pieces of the bill into Pop's hand.

For a moment the puncher stared at them.

"You was goin' to roll 'em in this handkerchief an' then they'd be O.K., wasn't you?" he asked.

"Yea, I *was*," Nick replied sardonically. "But the show's closed."

"That's all you had to do — just roll 'em up?"

"That's all," and Nick laughed again, harshly.

"Well, that seems easy. If you could do it, don't see why I can't. Now let's see. I put 'em in this way, an' fold the cloth. Then what?"

Nick did not answer. He strolled toward the door.

"Hey, Nick! what do I do now?"

"Make soup out of 'em," came the answer over Nick's shoulder.

"Hey, wait, Nick! Maybe it'll work! Stick around fer a second, will yuh? Maybe I can do it!"

"Yea, an' maybe cows can fly, too," Nick snorted. But he turned, never-theless, with a desire to see Pop's failure.

Carefully the old man rolled the handkerchief containing the pieces of the bill into a small ball. This he held in the palm of his hand for a moment.

"Now, she ought to work," he stated doubtfully. With a flip of his wrist he sent the handkerchief flying open. From its folds fluttered not the torn pieces he had put in, but — a ten dollar bill, whole and entire!

"What!"

Nick's eyes almost bulged from their sockets. Amazement was written large on his face. He leaned forward, breathing hard.

"There she is!" Pop shouted triumphantly. "Told you it 'ud work! All it needed was somebody to do it! Gus, there's yore tenner as good as new. Nick, yore a poluka. That's as easy as pie! She came right out, as easy as easy!"

Nick turned his head slowly, looking at Pop with awe. He blinked rapidly. Then, without a word, he stumbled to the door and disappeared.

Gus bent down and picked up his bill, a wide grin on his face. He bowed to Pop.

"From one artist to another — greetings," he snickered.

Pop returned the bow. Then, reaching for his back pocket, he drew out a thin volume. Silently he held it up, so that Roy and Teddy could read the name on it.

"Found it in Nick's foot-locker," he said simply. "Makes right interestin' readin'."

Teddy and Roy bent forward. Then, as they read the title, a roar of laughter burst from each. Long and loudly they laughed, for on the cover of the book were the words:

"A Hundred Ways to Amuse Your Friends."

CHAPTER XII

THE GIRLS ARE GONE

On Friday, the day that Teddy and Roy were to ride to the 8 X 8 for Belle and bring her home, a squadron of black, low-hung clouds marched over the mountains and began to discharge their ammunition of rain toward a thirsty earth. They were seemingly well stocked, for they held their position for three days, until, on the morning of the fourth, the sun dispersed them.

During the storm, the business of the ranch had practically come to a standstill, for there was little that could be done in wet weather. Besides that, the time before a fall round-up is always slack, the punchers spending most of their days repairing their outfits and doing odd jobs about the yard and the corral.

Nick Looker wasted many hours in deep thought over the trick Pop had played on him. Of course he found that his book had been taken from his foot-locker, but even then he remained somewhat in the dark. He simply could not fathom how Pop had turned the joke so cleverly. He took Roy and Teddy into his confidence, and they listened with grave faces to his tale of woe.

"If Pop was a clever scout, or something like that, I could understand it," Nick confessed. "But he's such a dumb galoot! I can't figure it nohow! There he stands, with a look on his map as innercent as a white-faced yearling, an' I walk right into his hands! Then he turns around an' gives me the royal razz. No sir, it's beyond me! Oh, I can guess how he did the trick all right, after he saw how in that book of mine. That ain't what's worryin' me. What I want to know is how he planned the whole busted business an' was Gus in with him. By golly, she's too many fer me!"

The two brothers, restraining their laughter, admitted they could not solve the problem for him, and, shaking his head, Nick walked away. It was many days before he could hear a laugh without staring with a suspicious scowl at the merry one.

The wind was strong at times and one extra heavy gust blew down several of the poles upon which the telephone wire was fastened. As a consequence, the phone was out of commission for several days. At the time nobody thought anything of this, for the local line was none too good and often went out of commission.

Although during the rain Roy and Teddy did no range riding, except one afternoon when the sun shone for a few hours, promising clear weather, only to disappear behind clouds again by evening, yet they were not idle. Together with their father, they went over all possible places the escaped rustlers might try to raid the herd and steal cattle, planning to fortify the weak spots against possible depredations. There were now five men riding herd, and Mr. Manley seriously considered adding another, but after a consultation with the boys, decided against it.

"Can't have 'em all out," he declared. "If that 'Reltsur' starts anything around the ranch, we don't want to be handicapped by lack of men. This time there'll be none of this 'man to man' stuff. I want no more trouble with that gang of hoss thieves, an' I'll let them alone if they'll stay their distance. But if they want to mix it —" and the man's eyes narrowed — "they'll get what they're lookin' for! At the first sign of trouble we ride 'em down, an' polish 'em off, if we have to. The sooner they learn that the new West has no place for rustlers an' gunmen, the better. In the old days —" He hesitated, and a smile trembled on his lips, but instantly his face grew grave again. "They're gone forever. We have no more time for chasin' hoss thieves all over the landscape. Besides, the men were different then.

"Do you suppose Gilly Froud would last a minute around a gang like Whitey Kunkle an' Mike Delnegro an' Lasher Pete? Huh! he'd be run off the reservation. Those waddies may have been tough, but they weren't cowards an' wouldn't plug a man without givin' him a chance to go fer his shootin' iron. But these birds!" His eyes flickered with contempt. "Why, they ain't even tough! They're just a bunch of sore-heads, afraid to take a man on unless he's tied hand an' foot and him in the light while they're shootin' from the dark! A fine gang! Sendin' a note sayin' I'd get mine if I didn't lay off 'em!

"Well, let 'em come! Maybe when the lazy cowards find out they can't blaze away from behind a brick wall or a barroom window, they'll change their minds about thinkin' they're bold, bad cattle rustlers!"

This was the longest speech the boss had made in many a moon. But it indicated his feelings in the matter, and left no doubt as to his intentions if "Reltsur" tried to make good his threat. Mr. Manley never looked for trouble, nor, indeed, did he meet it half way. It had to come up to his door and knock if it wanted to see him; but once it did that, the vicinity would not complain of lack of excitement for some time to come.

It was only natural that his two sons should inherit some of this steady, determined disposition of his, and Teddy and Roy had it in full measure. Still, Roy's was tempered with much of the gentleness of his mother, and, like her, he met the world with grave, understanding eyes. While he shared, in a measure, Teddy's wholehearted appreciation of a bit of horseplay, yet frequently he would see behind outward appearances and discover things which were lost to his brother's more superficial glance.

Yet, in the situation existing at the X Bar X Teddy himself found plenty of food for thought. His father had taken the warning signed "Reltsur" with a great deal more gravity than the younger boy had thought he would. This, in itself, was enough to convince Teddy that the matter could not be laughed off. To add to this, the several happenings before and after the visit of the night rider, while none of them significant in themselves, yet totaled into an aspect calling for consideration.

The lone horseman on Mica Mountain, the day of the slide, who rode with that slouch so reminiscent of another puncher. The delivery of the note. The escape of the rustlers from jail. The hoofbeats behind the car as the boys rode home from the 8 X 8. And, had they but known it, the figure lurking near the corral on that same bright moonlight night when the horses neighed and moved restlessly. All this presaged something.

Lucky that Froud, at least, was out of the way. Then a sudden thought struck Teddy, and he chuckled. Perhaps it was lucky for Froud, too, that he was safe in jail! Just before his capture he had knifed the head of the band of rustlers of which he was a member, so that he might take the leader's place and thus get a larger share of the booty for himself. He had left the man for dead, but, with a desperate effort, the leader, who named himself Brand, which was particularly appropriate, finally reached a cabin where Teddy and Roy had taken shelter from a storm. They had bound up Brand's wounds and later, out of thankfulness for their services, he had told them of a plan the rustlers had made to steal the cattle of the X Bar X. Then he left — left, possibly, to hunt Froud, who had knifed him. Thus it was well for Froud that he was still in safety behind prison bars.

Teddy's mind was revolving these thoughts during the time that the rain beat down upon the range, converting it into an ocean of mist, with the mountains sticking their heads out like the tall masts of ships. But at last a brisk wind arose, the clouds were blown away, and the sun greeted the dripping trees with a warm smile.

That afternoon Mrs. Manley asked Roy and Teddy to take a car to Peter Ball's place and bring Belle home.

"I'm afraid she may have outstayed her welcome already," their mother added, with a smile. "She may want to bring Nell and Ethel back with her. I don't suppose you boys will object?"

"Well, not very loudly, Mom," Teddy answered, with a laugh. "I know Roy won't, anyhow. I caught him using a rhyming dictionary the other day."

"Like fun you did!" his brother retorted, his face fiery red. "That was just an ordinary, plain, every-day dictionary! Where do you get that stuff — 'rhyming dictionary'? What would I do with a rhyming dictionary? What would be the sense of it? I don't even know how to use one — that is, not very well. And, anyway, that wasn't one! It was —"

"Whoa, baby! Tighten up that cinch-strap — you're slipping! Wow! Listen to him, Mom! He's going to be a politician! I can tell!"

"Well, it wasn't a rhyming dictionary," Roy grumbled, laughing a little. "And you'd better take a look at the car, Teddy. We don't want another puncture or another scare like — like — that landslide," he finished quickly. "What time shall we start, Mom?"

Mrs. Manley wanted them to leave as soon as possible, so they might get back before dark; so, making sure the auto was filled with gas and oil, they began their journey. After the storm, the air was cool and invigorating, and, as they rode along, Roy explained the theory of "low pressure areas" until Teddy remarked that he thought an area was a song from an opera. It took a minute for this to penetrate, but when it did Roy snorted in disgust and refused to say another word until Teddy hit an especially large bump, sending Roy flying toward the top of the car. Even then Roy's description of Teddy's driving had very little to do with opera.

"Wonder what the girls did during all that rainy weather," Teddy remarked, as they neared the 8 X 8.

"Curly was probably writing letters to you, which she forgot to send," Roy responded, with a grin. "Aside from that, I guess they talked. Somehow, girls seem to do that especially well."

"Think Nell and Ethel will come back with Belle?"

"Yep."

"Golly, you sure seem positive about it. How do you know?"

"Got a hunch."

Teddy drove on in silence for a moment.

"What'll you bet they won't be at home when we get there?" he said finally.

"What do you mean — that they'll be out riding? Well, we can wait. Bug Eye will probably be there, an' we can bat the sock with him for a while. Jimminy, I don't know what made me think he could have written that note — and him the one who helped us capture the rustlers, too! Well, we live and learn. I guess, after all, that message was just to scare us. Nothing will come of it. The rustlers are probably miles away from here by now, heading for Mexico. Chances are we'll never hear of them again. Come on, step on it. Mother said she wanted us back before dark."

As he depressed the accelerator, Teddy stole a look at his brother. Roy had expressed the very opposite of his former declarations! Did he really think the horse thieves had abandoned their plans for revenge? Well, maybe so. It seemed likely, now that all this time had passed without any sign of them. Teddy sank more deeply in the seat. If Roy wasn't worrying, certainly he should not!

A quarter of an hour more and they reached the yard of the 8 X 8. As Teddy and Roy alighted, they noticed that there was no sign of activity about the place. The yard was deserted.

"Told you they'd be out," Teddy asserted, as the boys walked toward the door of the ranch house.

"Riding, most likely. Guess Mrs. Ball is in, though."

Teddy rang the doorbell and waited. In a moment the door opened, and a large, jolly-faced woman greeted them with a smile.

"Come in, come in!" she said, beaming on them. "Glad you boys came over. Bug-Eye was saying only the other day that he wanted to ask you about a new kind of carburetor. Pete is out, but if you'll sit down I'll get you some milk and sandwiches. Guess you can eat?"

"Right the first time, Mrs. Ball," Roy answered, with a grin. "But don't go to any trouble. We've got to start right back — as soon as sis and Nell and Ethel are ready. They're out riding, I suppose?"

A puzzled look came over Mrs. Ball's face. She hesitated when halfway to the door, and turned.

"What do you mean, out riding?" she asked, curiously. "They're at your place, aren't they?"

"At our place!" Teddy echoed. He paled slightly. "I'm — I'm afraid I don't understand you, Mrs. Ball. Why should they be at our place?"

"Why, you sent for them! You don't mean to say —"

"Let's get this straight, Mrs. Ball," Roy said slowly. His voice trembled just a little. "Aren't Belle and Ethel and Nell here?"

"Why, of course not! Oh, what can have happened? Oh, my gracious! I don't know what I'm doing! I'm so turned around! Why, a man came Saturday in an auto with a note from your mother, saying he was to take the girls with him — the three of them! And they went, Belle, Ethel, and Nell — they went with him! Why, I thought he was from your place! Oh, my lands! what can have happened? The three girls — they're gone — they're gone!"

CHAPTER XIII

An Ultimatum

Just outside the house a whistle sounded. Neither Roy nor Teddy heard it. They stood facing Mrs. Ball, their faces a sickly white beneath their tan. Slowly Teddy's hands clenched until his nails dug into his palms. Roy took a quick breath, which sounded like a gasp in the silence of that room.

Mrs. Ball swayed slightly, and Roy took a swift step forward.

"It's — it's all right," he said uncertainly. "Don't — get excited. I think — I —"

"Gone!" The word seemed wrung from the woman's bloodless lips. "Belle — Ethel — Nell — gone! I tell you they're gone! Where — where — they're gone —"

She seemed about to faint, and Teddy and Roy sprang to her side. At that moment a step sounded in the doorway and a man's voice boomed a greeting, only to be cut off sharply as Peter Ball took in the scene with a rapid glance. When his wife saw him, she came to herself somewhat and flung herself sobbing into his arms.

"Oh, Pete!" she moaned, "something terrible has happened. The girls — our nieces — and Belle Ada — who were here —"

"Now, now, Sera, just take things easy," Mr. Ball soothed. He looked quickly at Roy and Teddy, a frantic question in his eyes.

"You see, Mr. Ball," Teddy stammered, "we thought Belle and the other girls were still here, and we came over to get them and Mrs. Ball told us that they had left for our place on Saturday with a man who had a note —"

"Do you mean to say he wasn't one of your father's men?" Mr. Ball demanded, holding his wife close and staring incredulously at the boys. "Why, he had a note from your mother! Sera — Sera —" He looked down at his wife. "Where is that note? Have you got it?"

"It's — it's upstairs," Mrs. Ball murmured, her voice choked with tears. Suddenly she straightened, and, with a determined motion, drew her hands over her eyes. "Wait here — I'll get it," and she hurried toward the stairs.

Roy fingered his hat uncertainly.

"I don't know what to say, Mr. Ball," he muttered. "We haven't heard from the girls and we thought they were still here. I can't imagine —"

Teddy gave a short laugh, and his brother and Mr. Ball turned to him in surprise. Then they saw that he was staring fixedly at the wall, a strained look on his face. The laugh had come from between clenched teeth.

"I've got an idea," Teddy said slowly. "I've got a hunch — and — and if it's true, I'll —" Suddenly he raised both hands and shouted:

"Pull a rotten trick like that, will you? The dirty thieves! Kidnappers! Girl stealers! We'll get ours, will we? Not this time! Reltsur! I know — I know —"

"Teddy!"

Roy seized his brother's arm in a grip of steel.

"Teddy, stop it! Teddy! Snap out of it now! You don't know anything! You're just guessing! Stop that yelling!"

Teddy put his hand to his head. For a moment he shook as though with the ague, then took a deep breath.

"I'm sorry," he muttered. "I — I didn't mean to shout. Didn't know what I was doing, I guess. Don't mind me —"

Mr. Ball stepped forward and laid a friendly hand on the boy's shoulder.

"I know just how you feel, son," he said kindly. "But don't get worked up. The girls may be all right. It may be just a joke, or — or something. Take it easy, son. When my wife comes down — Did you get it, Sera?" he broke off eagerly.

Silently his wife handed him a slip of paper. Mr. Ball glanced at it and passed it to Roy. Together the two boys stared at the writing.

It was short and addressed to Mrs. Peter Ball. It ran:

"This will introduce Jack Richmond, who is driving for us now. He has come to bring Belle Ada home. Can't Nell and Ethel visit with us for a while? We should love to have them. They can all pile in the car with Jack, and he'll bring them over to our ranch. Please say yes.

"BARBARA HAVENS MANLEY."

For a long moment the boys gazed at the note. Then Teddy reached out and took it from his brother's unresisting hand.

"That writing," he murmured, still with bent head. "It looks familiar. I've seen it before —" He glanced swiftly up. "Roy! do you recognize it? That capital R?"

Roy peered at the note again. Then his eyes narrowed.

"Reltsur!"

"That's who! The one who sent the note to dad! So, that's his game, is it? Well, he won't get far! The dog, I'll —" Teddy stopped, breathing hard. He lowered his voice.

"I hate to say it, Mr. Ball, but I think Belle and the others have been stolen — kidnapped!"

A shocked silence came over those in the room. It seemed too incredible. It was not to be believed that anything like this could happen. Why, only last week the three girls were standing in the garden just outside the window. Belle had picked a wild rose and had twined it in her lovely black hair. She and Nell and Ethel had stood there, as the boys approached, and Ethel had said "Want some nice, fresh —"

There, in the garden, were the roses. Their sweet scent drifted in through the open window. A light breeze sprang up, moving the screen door, so that the hinges creaked. Out in the yard a horse whinnied softly.

Peter Ball gulped noisily.

"Stolen, hey?" he said in a harsh voice. "You sure of that?"

"This note is written in the same hand that wrote a warning to dad," Roy was talking fast. "Two weeks ago, at night, a rider passed our bunkhouse, where Teddy and I and some of the boys were standing, and flung us a message tied to a stick. It said if dad pressed the charge against the rustlers, who were in jail at Hawley, he'd get his. Then we heard the rustlers had escaped. And now this —" He motioned toward the paper Teddy still held in his hand.

"The man who sent the note threatened your dad?" Mr. Ball demanded, a fierce frown on his face.

"That's what," Teddy answered in a dull voice. "And it looks like he'd made good, too. Got us standing flat-footed," he added bitterly.

"The man who came here was a — a rustler?" Mrs. Ball gasped.

"Now, Sera, just take it easy," Mr. Ball boomed. He patted his wife's shoulder awkwardly. "Suppose you have a lie-down on the couch for a while? Remember what the doctor said about your heart. Boys, you and I —"

"I won't lie down!" Mrs. Ball exclaimed, her face flushed. "I'm going after those kidnappers, that's what I'm going to do! Pete, you get me a gun! No man is going to steal three girls right from under my nose — not while I'm healthy! You just forget about my heart! It's as good as it ever was! I guess I haven't lived in the West all my life for nothing! I guess I haven't forgotten how to shoot, either! Pete, I'm going to ride with you!" She pushed back a loose strand of hair and stood gasping for breath.

Pete Ball shook his head slowly.

"No, Sera," he said gently. "I'm afraid not. I know how much you want to, but some one has got to stay here and take charge of things. You can do more to help in that way than any other. It's just possible that the girls might escape and make their way back here. You see what I mean, don't you, Sera?" He looked at her anxiously.

After a moment Mrs. Ball nodded.

"Guess you're right, Pete," she said heavily. "I was crazy to think you could be bothered with a woman along. But when I think of Nell, Ethel and Belle being taken by that bunch of gunmen to heaven knows where, I — I —"

Then she stopped and walked over to her husband. She rested her hands on his shoulders and looked in his eyes.

"Pete," she said in a low voice, "listen to me! You know I love you better than anything in the world. We've been together now for twenty-six years. We've seen this old ranch grow up from a little cattle farm to a place we can be proud of. We've had lots of hard times, you and I, and we've weathered them all. I'd rather die myself than have anything happen to you. But now —" her voice rose, and took on a vibrant tone — "Pete, bring back those girls! They were our guests. They were under our very roof, under our protection, and I love every one of them like a daughter. If you have to give your own life to do it, Pete, bring — back — those — girls!"

CHAPTER XIV

OFF ON THE CHASE

Quite simply and unaffectedly, Mr. Ball kissed his wife on the forehead. He said not a word, but stood for a moment looking down at her. Then, motioning to Roy and Teddy, he made for the door.

"We'll get 'em," Roy declared brokenly. "We'll get 'em, I vow it! Teddy —"

For a moment tears welled up in the older youth's eyes, but they were tears of sudden, violent emotion, and Roy wiped them away, unashamed. He saw his brother standing in the center of the room, shoulders drooping, a dull, leaden look of deep despair on his face. When Roy touched his arm he started.

"Teddy, let's be going," the boy said softly.

"Belle!" Teddy muttered, "Belle gone —"

Suddenly Mrs. Ball saw that her speech had brought the blow home to the boys with deadening force. She shook her head sadly and grasped an arm of each.

"Buck up!" she exclaimed firmly. "Teddy, you're not going to weaken now, are you? Come on, Pete is waiting for you. I'll telephone your folks — the linemen just finished their work on this section and we can use the phone again — and send Bug Eye over with some men to your ranch right away. We'll be so hot on the trail of those rustlers they'll wish they'd never heard of the West! Why, you'll have your sister back within twenty-four hours! We'll rake this whole prairie with a fine tooth comb! We'll get 'em, no matter where they hide! You listen to me — I know what I'm talking about! Look up now and ride after 'em, boys! Go get 'em!"

Teddy came to life as though he had touched a live wire. Then he threw back his shoulders and his eyes blazed. The blood returned to his face with a rush.

"We'll get 'em!" he exclaimed harshly. "I don't care where they hide — they can't get away! Roy, let's go! We'll ride 'em down, wherever they are! Good-bye, Mrs. Ball — don't worry! Roy! Come on!"

The boys ran across the room. The door slammed shut behind them. There was a slight jar as they leaped down the steps. In another moment the roar of a motor sounded, the cutout on full. Mrs. Ball rushed to the window, and saw the auto, with her husband and the boys in it, speed madly up the road. For a moment she stood there, watching the cloud of dust settle as the car disappeared over the hill. Then she covered her face with her hands and sobbed:

"Let them find them, O Lord! Let them find them! I haven't asked for very much up to now; but please, Lord, let them bring the girls home safely! Send their sister back to those two dear boys and my nieces back to me! Please! Oh, please!"

Gradually her sobs subsided. Then, calm-eyed and determined, she went to the telephone. Mr. Ball had not misplaced his trust in her.

The occupants of the car which was burning up the road between the X Bar X and the 8 X 8 were, for the most part, silent, sunk deep within their thoughts. Teddy was driving automatically, his eyes fixed upon the road, his mind spinning with tangled ideas. The rustlers had made good their threat. His father's fears had been realized. But in what a fashion! None of them had anticipated anything like this! Even now it was hard to realize. That there could be men in this country who would stoop to a scoundrel's trick of this sort! If they had only had some intimation of what was about to occur! They had imagined the rustlers might make trouble of some kind — steal the cattle or even shoot them down from ambush. Better, far better, that the whole herd be killed than this!

What would his father say? And mother! Teddy blinked his eyes rapidly. Viciously he pressed the accelerator to the floor and the car shot ahead.

"Not wastin' any time," Mr. Ball declared, leaning forward from his seat in the rear. Teddy shook his head, but did not trust himself to reply. He was not sure his voice would be quite steady.

Roy turned to Mr. Ball.

"Will your wife be all right alone? She won't —"

"She's a thoroughbred," Mr. Ball answered shortly. "After she's had her little cry she'll be as cool and collected as any man. Your folks will know about it before we get there, Roy, an' Mrs. Ball will get our bunch together an' send 'em on over. Bet you she'll remember to send an extra horse by Bug Eye, too, for me. She's a great little woman — a great little woman —" His voice trailed off into silence, and once more the three sat staring intently at the road ahead.

To Roy's mind there came the picture of another ride taken not so very long ago, in from Eagles. That was the day their horses had been stolen and Nell and Ethel had been in the car with them. Roy remembered how Nell had exclaimed excitedly when they reached Bitter Cliff lookout, that high, mountainous point halfway between the town and their ranch. Eagerly he had pointed out the 8 X 8, where the two girls were going to visit. And that had been but a few short months ago! Now — now —

"Looks like rain," Teddy said, in a voice so low Roy scarcely heard him.

"Can't tell —" Roy scanned the horizon with obvious carefulness. "Those clouds aren't quite black enough for rain. Guess we've had our share of it."

As if it made any difference! Yet it was something to talk about, something else than Belle and Ethel and Nell. Worrying would do no good. They must keep calm and work coolly and determinedly, rather than allow the rage in their hearts to seep through and warp their judgment.

Roy glanced at Teddy out of the corner of his eye. He noticed that the boy's face was set in stern lines and that his eyes never wavered from the road. Small bunches of muscles stood out just above his jawbone, like solid hickory-nuts. Teddy was all right. Almost, Roy could see the cold, silent determination within his brother's mind. The anger which possessed Teddy was a white anger — the kind that drives men on over all obstacles, oblivious of pain, of danger, until they have won through. Roy bent slightly to the left until his shoulder touched his brother's. A sort of electric current passed through the two boys. They were together, shoulder to shoulder, nothing could stop them! In that moment Roy knew they would never rest until the three girls had been found.

When the car pulled into the yard of the X Bar X, Mr. Manley hurried from the house and came toward it. Silently he held out his hand to Peter Ball, then, as the boys alighted, he drew nearer and threw an arm about each for a moment.

"Mrs. Ball telephoned," he said quietly. "Glad we got the line mended in time. I'm having Nick and Gus get the horses ready. Mrs. Ball said that Bug Eye and four other men were on their way over with a bronc for you, Pete. We'll start right out as soon as they come."

"Where's mother?" Teddy asked quickly.

"In the house, son. She's all right. Want to see her?"

Both boys nodded and walked toward the steps, while the two men talked together in low tones.

The boys found their mother sitting calmly by the window. As she saw them she smiled slightly, and Roy and Teddy drew deep breaths of relief. They had been afraid — even more than they would admit to themselves — of how she would bear up. But her smile told them they need have no fear. She was true blue, a real woman of the West. She would face the trouble with the rest of them and stand her share of it. Lovingly she kissed her sons and looked searchingly into their eyes. What she found there seemed to satisfy her, for she said gently:

"Your father has been waiting for you, boys. We know all about it — Mrs. Ball telephoned. Teddy — Roy — it came suddenly, didn't it? But we mustn't worry too much. I know they're all right! Somehow, I am sure of it. Nothing will happen to them. I've said a little prayer, and my Friend hasn't failed me yet!" she finished brightly. "Now you must hurry, boys. Put on heavy clothes — you may have to ride far and long. I'll see you before you leave. There!" and she kissed them again.

"You're — you're all right, Mother?" Roy faltered.

"All right? Of course I'm all right!" her eyes expressed well simulated surprise. "Why shouldn't I be? We'll have them back before to-morrow night!"

"That's what Mrs. Ball said!" Teddy exclaimed, a light coming into his eyes. "And I believe we shall, Mother! Dad knows this country like a book, and so do we. By golly, we'll show 'em what chance they have against a bunch of real Westerners — those New York sneak thieves, who think they're bad men! We'll track 'em down an' salivate 'em!"

"Good!" exclaimed Mrs. Manley firmly. "That's the way I like to hear my boys talk! You find them — and — and *salivate* them!"

As the boys returned to the yard, a great weight seemed lifted from their hearts. That it had fallen to the heart of their mother, they did not know. Her willing spirit had taken much of the burden from their souls, embracing it as her own. How could they know that it had passed from them to her with their mother's kiss!

Now they felt confident, sure of success. Their steps were firm, their hands steady. And as their father saw them, he sensed the wonder that had been performed and silently blessed his wife. In that hour she may have lost her boys, but she had gained two men.

In the midst of preparations for the start, Bug Eye and four other men arrived. They had forced their horses to the limit, and the ponies stood panting and covered with sweat in the ranch yard.

"Made good time," Mr. Manley said to Bug Eye as the puncher dismounted.

"Had to," was the grim answer. "When Mrs. Ball told us what had happened we saddled up and rushed over here pronto. My boss around?"

"Talking to Mrs. Manley. He'll be out in a minute. Can you start as soon as your broncs get rested, Bug Eye?"

"Sure can," Bug Eye replied grimly. "An' we're not holdin' back any, either. What's the plan, Mr. Manley?"

Before answering, Mr. Manley called his men around him. Mr. Ball had come out of the ranch house and was standing with the rest. Of the X Bar X men there were Nick Looker, Pop Burns, Gus Tripp and Nat Raymond, besides, of course, Mr. Manley and Roy and Teddy. Thus, with the four men who had ridden over from the 8 X 8 with Bug Eye, there was quite an assemblage in the yard, waiting for Mr. Manley to speak.

He held up his hand, and the talk died down. The men leaned forward eagerly. They sensed from Mr. Manley's face that a serious moment was at hand. All of them had heard something of what had happened, yet they anxiously awaited the orders of the boss of the X Bar X Ranch.

"Boys," Mr. Manley began, "this ain't goin' to be much of a speech. I don't feel in the mood for talkin', an' I guess you ain't hankerin' to stand there listenin', either. You all know that my daughter and Nell Willis and Ethel Carew were stayin' at the 8 X 8. Last Saturday a man in an auto comes up to Pete Ball's place with a note, sayin' that he's to bring the girls back with him. The note was signed with my wife's name." He paused for a moment, then went on:

"My wife didn't send no such letter. This man took the three girls with him, to bring home, as they thought. That was Saturday. To-day is Monday. We haven't heard from the girls since." Once more he paused, and his eyes roved over the men about him. Then he continued:

"I guess most of you heard about the message I got a week or so ago, sayin' I'd get mine for pushin' the charge against those rustlers we rounded up. That note was signed 'Reltsur,' and Roy an' Teddy say the letter Mrs. Ball got was in the same handwritin'. Those rustlers are out of jail now — they made a getaway. Men, it looks bad — it looks *bad*!"

"You think that gang of hoss thieves did this job, boss?" Nick broke in.

"Sure seems so, Nick! An' I'll lay money that they did, too! They have it in for me. An' I heard they have two or three gunmen from the East with 'em. Yep, that's who we've got to look for, men — this guy Reltsur."

There was silence for a moment, then a voice asked:

"You say some geezer drove up last Satiday an' took three girls away from the 8 X 8, boss?"

All turned to the speaker. He was one of the men who had ridden over with Bug Eye, a new hand, Bug Eye explained later.

"That's what," Mr. Manley answered sharply. "You know anything about it?"

"Wall, I'll tell you what I see," the man drawled. "I was ridin' in toward the 8 X 8 about sundown on Satiday. You see, I don't know this country so well, an' I was sort of huggin' the road, so I wouldn't —"

"Never mind that, man. Spill it — explain later!" Mr. Ball interrupted.

"Right. Well, as I was sayin', I was pretty close to the road. All of a sudden I hears a car comin' an' I thinks I'll just hang around an' see who it is. So I jumps my bronco behind a tree an' waits."

In the pause that followed, the forced breathing of the men could be plainly heard. All eyes were glued on the puncher, who went calmly on:

"Pretty soon I see a car down the road. As she comes closer, I noticed there were five people in it."

"Five!" Teddy exclaimed.

"Yep. There were three girls, a man drivin', an' an old woman, who sure looked like a Mex, sittin' in the front seat beside him."

"A woman!" exclaimed Mr. Manley.

"Why didn't you speak of this before?" asked Pete Ball, a bit sharply.

"Didn't get no chance, boss," was the calm answer. "I been out ridin' fence ever since you hired me, which was soon after I rode in on Satiday. I didn't hear nothin' about no kidnappin' till jes' now on th' way over, an' then I begun puttin' two an' two together. For all I knowed, them folks in the auto might 'a' been a picnicin' party."

"That's right," agreed Mr. Manley. "But it's lucky that you happened to see them, cowboy!"

"I hope it'll turn out so. I'd sure have mentioned it afore if I'd knowed what it meant. But I was sent for in a hurry to join what I thought was a bunch jest takin' after rustlers, and it wasn't until I heard the young ladies mentioned jest now that I remembered about that crowd in the auto. The driver, a mean-lookin' sort of cuss, seemed in a pronto rush, an' the old crone was hoverin' over the girls like a hen with three chicks."

"Then they must be goin' to hold Belle and the others for ransom. Boys, if we have to, we'll pay it — but we'll give them a fight first! At any rate, I believe the girls are safe for a while. Go on, man, which way did the car head?" asked Mr. Manley.

"Well, now, I was just tryin' to think. There's a cut around here somewhere, only I can't think of the name of it. Let's see — somethin' like Lightnin' Gorge or —"

"Thunder Canyon?" Teddy broke in eagerly.

"That's it! Thunder Canyon! That's where they was headed for! An' they were sure steppin' along, too. Thunder Canyon! That's the place."

Mr. Manley turned to the others. His eyes were narrowed and his hand rested on the gun which hung at his side.

"You men get set," he said tersely. "We start right away. Each man take rations enough to last him for three or four days an' bring plenty of ammunition. We do no more foolin' around! From now on we ride them rustlers till we get 'em."

Instantly every one was astir. Saddles and guns were looked over carefully and small bags of flour, bacon, and tea were prepared. The boys and their father said a fond good-bye to Mrs. Manley, who, when she heard of the puncher's story of the other woman in the car, felt greatly relieved. After all, the worst that could happen would be that the rustlers would hold the girls until Mr. Manley consented to do their bidding, whatever it might be. They would never dare to kill three girls in cold blood.

71

At last all was in readiness. The party was mounted, guns showing conspicuously in saddle holsters, and the men awaited the word to start.

Mr. Manley ran from the house and vaulted into the saddle. He looked quickly about him, to see that all the men were there. Then he nodded.

"All right," he said laconically. "Let's go! Head for Thunder Canyon."

"Right, boss," answered Gus Tripp softly, and the others nodded.

In that calm fashion started the ride after the rustlers. No shouting, no raking of ponies' sides with spurs to send them into a leaping run. Just a bunch of punchers riding out of a ranch yard, as though they were on their way to a round-up.

Yet within the heart of every man there was a fierce, unconquerable purpose — to find the jailbirds and to "polish 'em off."

72

CHAPTER XV

AN UNEXPECTED CLEW

The trail to Thunder Canyon lay through a region noted for its treacherous footings and short, stubby clumps of mesquit grass that might conceal a hole just deep enough to break a pony's leg.

Swinging from the road, the riders entered this desolate tract and proceeded up a gentle slope, dotted here and there with trees burned almost leafless by summer suns. Here the land lay pitifully open to the brazen sky, long since beaten into submission and now venturing only half-heartedly to produce any protective vegetation. This was a land of exile, shunned and avoided by the surrounding territory. It was a field apart.

A dull haze covered the sun as the punchers rode stolidly on. Teddy turned to glance at his brother, who was loping along in the rear.

"Making the grade, Roy?" he called, and threw his head slightly to one side. Roy correctly interpreted the motion, and urged his pony until he was close to Teddy.

"How did that story we heard strike you?" Teddy asked, looking about him to see that no one was listening. The noise of creaking saddles and the beat of the horses' feet on the baked earth prevented the boy's voice from carrying far.

"Ike Natick's?" Roy countered.

"Don't know his name. The puncher who came over with Bug Eye."

"His name is Natick. He's a new hand. Bug Eye says he hasn't been with their outfit very long. But he says he's a good man, and I think he is, too. He impresses me as being all cowboy."

Teddy nodded.

"Just wanted to get your idea. I like him O. K. myself. Kind of long and stringy, but he's built like a rawhide whip. So you think we can depend on him?"

"I think so, Teddy. Anyway, we've got to. He's the only one who knows anything about this business, and it's nothing more than pure, dumb luck that he knows as much as he does. He spoke of a woman being in the car. I'm sure glad of that, but I wonder who she could have been?"

"Some half-breed probably, carried along to take care of the girls. Those rustlers are not exactly fools, I guess, and they know that if anything serious happened their lives wouldn't be worth a plugged nickel. I reckon the girls will be treated fairly, all right, and I'm not worried about that. But

I can't stand the thought of those jailbirds holding Belle and Ethel and Nell captives while they dictate terms to us! That sort of gets under my skin, by golly! Then, too, unless we find them soon, we can't tell what —"

He pulled Flash aside to avoid a sharp depression and left his sentence unfinished. But Roy understood. He knew that they could not afford to delay, as the rustlers might become desperate and determine to abandon the girls to their fate rather than risk capture red-handed. Haste was imperative. While the girls were in the hands of gunmen and horse thieves they were in dire peril.

As the riders proceeded, they left behind that deserted waste and came into a more fertile country. They were nearing Thunder Canyon, through which ran a turbulent stream, and the nourishment derived from this water changed the grasses from a lifeless brown to a soft green. They made better speed now, the footing being much surer.

Before them rose a high mountain. They were to skirt this, for along its side was Thunder Canyon. Other mountains bordered the gulch, but these could not yet be seen. At the foot of the rise Mr. Manley called a halt.

"Natick!" he shouted, "ride up here a second, will you?"

The puncher complied, and stood near Roy and Teddy, who had approached their father and Mr. Ball.

"Right over there lies Thunder Canyon," Mr. Manley declared, and pointed.

Ike Natick grunted.

"I know it, boss. An' that's the place I mean. Somewhere in there you'll find those girl-stealin' gunmen."

"Yea?" Mr. Manley looked at him sharply. "What makes you so sure, Natick?"

"I ain't sure, boss; but I got a hunch. An' my hunches usually turn out pretty good. Besides that, it wasn't so far from here that I saw the car comin' this way. Don't that road to the 8 X 8 wind past those hills over there?"

"That's what," Pop Burns, who was listening, answered. "She runs right past them hills."

"Then I'm sure right," Ike Natick drawled. "That auto come into this here canyon. Course, they may have switched to horses later, 'cause the ground around here ain't none too good fer a car. I don't know nothin' about that. But you hear me, boss, an' head fer that there cut."

Pete Ball turned to Mr. Manley.

"I think he knows what he's talking about, Bardwell," he said in a low voice. "Ike hasn't been with me long, but I've found he's a born puncher, an' he sure knows the West. I'm in favor of takin' his advice an' searchin' that gorge."

74

For a moment the owner of the X Bar X ranch sat silent, thinking. He took his corncob pipe from his shirt pocket and stuck it, unlit, between his teeth.

"I'll agree with you, Pete," he said finally. "Pop, come here! You know more about Thunder Canyon than any man of us — or you should. Is there any place in it that might do for a stronghold for rustlers?"

"I'll say there is, boss!" Pop replied loudly. "The Sholo Caves near Gravestone Falls! I helped route a gang from there when I was ridin' fer yore father, boss. An' we had some job, let me tell you! We'd never have gotten 'em loose if one of their men hadn't welched and let us past. But we found out one thing — that the only way to really get a bunch out of those caves is to come at 'em from both sides of the canyon at once. The men on the other side keep 'em covered while those on this side stick 'em up. If we'd only knowed that when we had our fight, it would've turned out different. As it was, most of the rustlers got away. Me, I was with the party that —"

"Thanks, Pop," Mr. Manley said quickly, forestalling any attempt at one of the long speeches for which the veteran puncher was famous. "That tells us what we want to know. We head for Sholo Caves, men! Teddy, Roy, listen to me! You two are goin' to take the side with the caves on with Nick, Gus Tripp, an' Bug Eye. Pete an' I will ride across from you with the other men. We've got to keep in touch with each other. I guess you've been through Thunder Canyon before, boys?"

"Sure we have, Dad," Roy answered. "Though there are some parts of it pretty wide. If we can stay opposite each other till we get to the narrow part, we'll be all right."

Mr. Manley nodded in approval.

"That's what I've been thinkin'," he said. "But we have to chance that, I guess. You keep up the same pace we took comin' over here, an' I'll do likewise. When we get to the Falls, where she's narrow, we ought to be pretty near opposite each other. Anyway, we'll wait there until we get together. Anybody want to ask any questions before we start?"

The men were silent. The only questions they would ask would be of their guns — that they might not miss when the time came for action.

Before separating, the boys shook hands with their father. The grips were momentary, but they were firm, and told of sentiments which were more easily sensed than spoken. Each knew the danger he was about to face, and realized that this was the last time he might see the other alive. Certainly, there was the possibility of a tragic end to this serious business. Men who would kidnap girls would not hesitate to shoot to kill if the occasion arose.

Hence the boys knew well to what they were riding. Yet rather than hesitation, there was about them an eagerness which welcomed whatever might befall. Their sister was somewhere in that canyon. They were going to find her and Nell and Ethel, and not all the bullets ever moulded would prevent them!

"Good luck, boys," Mr. Manley said, as he sat quietly in his saddle a moment before starting. "Keep your powder dry an' your guns clean."

Those who heard him seemed to feel the old West rush upon them — the West with pistols leveled and eyes narrowed, the West that had produced a man like the boss of the X Bar X.

"Don't shoot unless you have to. But remember that Belle is in there, an', if you have to shoot, don't waste no bullets. I guess that's all."

He chirped to his pony. The boys did the same, and the father and his two sons separated, riding back to back. Behind Teddy and Roy come Nick Looker, Gus Tripp, and Bug Eye. The others were with Mr. Manley.

The canyon opened out before them. Mr. Manley's party had already entered it and were lost to sight behind the trees which bordered its edge.

Teddy and Roy looked down. At the bottom of the cut they could hear the faint tinkle of the running stream. From this rivulet the sides of rock rose perfectly straight, like the walls of two huge buildings. Then, higher up, the canyon gradually broadened, making a sort of V. Along the top edge of this V rode the boys, while towering over them, the taller mountains reared. It was a gorge within a gorge.

As Teddy's eyes swept over the tremendous expanse his heart faltered for a moment in sudden despair. How were they ever to find the girls in this place? The task was hopeless!

Then he remembered his mother's words:

"They'll be with us before to-morrow night!"

Touching Flash with his spurs, Teddy rode on.

CHAPTER XVI

A WOMAN THREATENS

"Yore dad took this mighty well," Nick declared, riding close to Roy. Teddy, Gus and Bug Eye drew up in the rear.

"He never does show much of what's going on inside him," Roy answered slowly. "You notice he didn't say hardly anything on the way over. Dad's hard hit, I know that. And — and so are we." He turned his head away for a moment and stared long and hard at something on the other side of the rugged canyon.

Nick moved uneasily in his saddle. At a time like this he was speechless. He did not know what he could say to console his friend, for his own heart was none too happy. His lips opened, but words would not come.

To punchers on the X Bar X, the ranch was as much a home as a place to work. Troubles were shared equally. Mr. Manley treated his men not like employees, but as friends who were helping him, and the boys appreciated this attitude.

Now that this cruel misfortune had come to the Manley family, every cowboy on the ranch felt it. Belle was loved and respected by every man on the place. Sing Lung, the cook, not excepted. When word had gone around that Belle had been kidnapped, a hot rage filled the hearts of the inmates of the bunk-house. Belle — little Belle, she of the raven black hair and laughing eyes — taken by rustlers! At first there had been a wild rush for horses and guns were out and ready in a moment. But cooler heads prevailed, and finally the boys had come to Mr. Manley, offering themselves quite simply for whatever he planned to do, whether it meant facing a rain of lead or not. He had thanked them huskily and told them to make ready.

These thoughts were running through Nick's mind as he rode along. If it was that they were to see Belle no more, if she were killed by the gunmen — He moved from side to side, as a caged animal moves. They'd run those jailbirds down, if it took them all their lives! And when they found them —

"Reckon there'll be any scrappin'?" Gus drawled, watching Teddy guide Flash carefully over bad ground.

"Expect so." The boy looked casually at the gun in his saddle holster. "Shots will make an awful roar in this canyon. Gus, what would happen to a man who fell that far?" He looked down toward the bottom of the dark space beneath him.

"Nothin' — that is, nothin' that he'd know about," Gus answered promptly. "Why, ain't aimin' to jump, are yuh?"

"Not any." Teddy laughed shortly. "But those caves, as I remember, are pretty close to the edge. Might be that one of those gunmen would lose his balance, accidental like, and slip. I was just wondering."

Gus nodded.

"Such might happen. Get a better view of it if a man was to watch the fall from the rear."

"That's what I was thinking." Teddy called to his brother. "Say, Roy, let's cut over to the right. The going is easier there, and we can move faster."

Roy considered this for a moment. He had not heard Teddy's conversation with Gus. Bug Eye explained matters in no uncertain terms, however, and Roy soon saw the advisability of approaching the caves from the rear. "But we don't want to lose touch with dad," he stated. "When the action starts, he's to take a stand on the other side of the canyon."

"An' pop away at us?" Nick asked wonderingly.

"Hum," Roy pulled his pony to a halt and pushed back his hat. "That's a point, Nick. Now let's see. Those caves, if I remember rightly, though I haven't been through here in three years, are almost at the end of this canyon. How about it?"

"Check."

"How many of 'em are there?"

"Well, I can't just say. No one knows exactly, 'cause they haven't all been explored. But I got a sort of idea they're all connected, somehow."

"Now if we ride in from the rear, as you said, Teddy, and dad's gang starts to shoot from the other side, it's going to be mighty uncomfortable for us. Nope, we'll have to stick close to the edge of the gorge. Then, when we get nearer, we can decide on our plan of action. But, golly, maybe the rustlers aren't there at all! We may be all wrong. At any rate, it's the only clew we have, so we may as well go by it. Anybody got any other suggestions?"

"We might send a man ahead when we get there to sound things out," Bug Eye said.

"I was counting on that. Teddy or I will reconnoiter and report back. If we only could make sure that we're going right! All this time, while we're in here, the thieves may be —" Roy stopped, and shook his head.

"But what can we do?" Teddy asked helplessly. "Natick said he saw the car head this way and Pop claims those caves are about the only place around here that the outlaws could use for a stronghold. If we're wrong, we'll have to start over again, that's all. It may take time, but we've simply got to sit tight and work our way over every possible spot where they could have hidden the girls. And we'll get 'em — we'll get 'em, by jinks!"

"I'll tell a maverick we will!" Roy burst out. "Come on, boys, let's hit it up!"

"How far is that narrow place from here, Nick, where we were going to see dad?" asked Teddy.

"Oh, quite a piece yet."

Once more they started, in single file now, for the trail was getting narrower. As they rounded a bend they caught sight of the stream below, which up to this time had been hidden by an overhanging ledge. They were riding downward now, and gradually they approached the bottom of the cut. But a little farther on they hit an up-grade where the path hugged the side of the rock so closely that the boys had to proceed with infinite caution. Their ponies were sure-footed, however, and they passed this dangerous spot without a mishap.

"Sun's goin' down," Bug Eye remarked, after a while.

No one replied to this, each man contenting himself with a single glance toward the west. They had expected to spend at least one night in the gorge, but Roy hoped they would get in touch with his father before darkness overtook them. They might easily lose track of each other if they tried to travel after nightfall, as the woods on the other side of the canyon were heavy and deep.

"See anything of the other gang?" Teddy asked, when they had ridden for some time in silence.

The others shook their heads. They were watching the opposite side eagerly, but the trees prevented them from obtaining a view of any riders that might be across from them. Besides, the gorge widened here, and they scarcely expected to see their companions until they reached the narrow part near Gravestone Falls, which was still a long ride ahead.

"If they get there before we do they'll wait," Roy remarked. "Dad wants us to be all together when we come in sight of the caves. He'll be a mighty disappointed man if Ike's hunch turns out wrong."

"So'll we all," Teddy agreed, with something strangely like a sigh. The long ride had given the boys ample time to think, which was the worst thing in the world for them. They needed action, and more than one man among them felt his hand wandering down toward the gun on his saddle or his hip. Thinking about the girls seemed to bring all sorts of wild fancies to the mind, though both Roy and Teddy were wise enough to know they must not harbor thoughts of failure. Worry would only use up their energy, and they would need all of that later.

Presently Roy, who was leading, held up his hand. Those behind him halted their horses and peered ahead.

"Remember this place, Nick?" the boy asked.

The puncher slowly shook his head.

"No, I don't, Roy. Seems like it's been widened since I rode over here last. As I remember it, this here path led right along the edge. Now she branches out, kind of."

They had come to a clearing on the side of the canyon. For a short space in front of them the ground was bare of bushes and trees, as though it had been purposely cleared. Motioning the others to follow, Roy rode on. A moment later, those behind Roy gave an exclamation.

"What's up, Roy?" Teddy asked quickly, springing his horse forward.

Roy pointed in silence. Just within the fringe of trees on the very edge of the clearing was a small cabin. Smoke was issuing from the chimney. And as the boys watched, a woman, old, stooped, and white-haired, her face creased with lines, came to the door.

"Mex!" whispered Nick excitedly.

To their surprise the woman suddenly disappeared into the hut. Roy started to urge his pony forward. Then quickly he pulled the reins taut, bringing Star to a halt.

The woman had come to the door again, and the boys could see her mouth twisted in rage. Her shoulders were thrown back and her eyes blazed. In her hands she held a long-barreled rifle, and, as the riders remained motionless, she lifted and leveled it with a steady hand.

CHAPTER XVII

CAPTIVES

The auto containing the three girls came to a dead stop. The driver turned to his companion, an old woman in a dress resembling a Gypsy's gown.

"This the place, Cleopatra?"

The woman nodded. Then she turned on him fiercely.

"My name Clovita! You no call me that other. Clovita my mother's name, and her mother's name before her. You no —"

"All right, all *right*! I'll call you Clove for short. That do? *Cloves* would just about suit you."

The woman made no reply, but, instead, turned and gazed stolidly at the three girls who sat in the rear seat and who were listening to this conversation with wildly beating hearts. Half an hour ago they had known that the man driving was not taking them home, but he had put them off with excuses that he had to stop some place first. Now Belle leaned forward and looked at him squarely.

"Mr. Richmond," she said firmly, "we want to know the meaning of this. We are not going home. This is nowhere near the X Bar X. Where are you taking us?"

"Well, now, I wouldn't just say you're not goin' home," the man drawled. "Let's say you're not goin' home yet. That sounds better. Now what else did you want to know?"

Belle felt the blood leave her face. She turned to the others.

"Don't be frightened," she said in a low voice. "He may be just trying to scare us. He won't dare keep us away long. Dad would kill him!"

"He would, hey?" The man laughed nastily. "So sure of that, Miss Spitfire? Maybe there's others around that can do a little killin' on their own hook."

Ethel gave a slight scream and began to tremble. Nell, taking her cue from Belle, clenched her teeth and remained silent.

The man spoke to the woman at his side.

"When were they coming?"

"T'ree 'clock."

"Well, it's four now. Sure this is the right place? If you're foolin' me, I'll —"

"Listen!"

The man bent his head sideways. In the distance sounded the beat of horses, evidently traveling toward the car, as the noise increased rapidly. The woman, not troubling to speak, jerked one thumb in the direction of the approaching ponies. The man nodded.

Belle, taking her courage in both hands, suddenly alighted from the car. She saw, out of the corners of her eyes, that the man had opened the door on his side and had slid himself out a bit from under the steering wheel. Belle knew that any attempt at escape would be met with instant violence, and she had no notion of giving this man an opportunity of tying her up. She simply stood by the side of the car and looked about her.

The place they had come to was familiar. It was the entrance to Thunder Canyon. Belle felt her heart give a jump of anxiety, for this was many miles from the X Bar X. She had known that something unusual was happening as soon as the car had stopped and had taken on the old woman, whom the driver explained by saying she was a relative of one of the cowboys and was going over to see him.

The woman, thinking such subterfuge unnecessary, had cackled shrilly, only to be silenced by a fierce frown from the man. It was then that Belle realized the turn affairs had taken. But she had refrained from alarming Nell and Ethel, both because it would be useless and because she hoped that if their driver could be lulled into thinking his motives were unsuspected, the girls might have a chance to escape. For it was certain that Richmond was no puncher on the X Bar X.

It had all happened so casually and so naturally that it was some time before the girls had become suspicious. The man had called at the 8 X 8 in the flivver with a note which Belle Ada was certain had been sent by her mother. The explanation, too, was natural.

The girls, eager for a change, had hurriedly packed and gotten in the car, chatting merrily and not paying much attention to the driver who, it was remembered now, had regarded them grimly as he drove off with them.

So merry had the trio been, anticipating much fun with Roy and Teddy at the Manley ranch, that they scarcely noted the direction taken by the driver. It was not until he stopped at a hut in a lonely place and the gaudily attired woman came out that Belle Ada glanced at Ethel and Nell strangely.

Then, with the woman in the car with them, had followed a long ride with suspicions increasing.

Belle realized that they were in a serious predicament — just how serious she could not yet tell, for, except for the knowledge that the driver was not connected with the X Bar X Ranch and that the note had been a forgery, the girl was as much in the dark as ever. But she did not lose heart.

Swiftly she glanced about her. Those hoofbeats were coming closer, and she knew if an escape were to be attempted, it must be soon.

"Mr. Richmond," Belle said slowly, turning toward the front seat, "I suppose it is useless to ask you for an explanation."

Before the man answered, he hitched up his belt, and Belle saw the butt of a revolver protruding over the door of the car. She pretended not to notice, and waited for his reply.

"What's the matter — ain't you comfortable?" the man countered. "I even brought Cleopatra along to — all right, Clovita, then! Don't go bitin' my ear off. I say I brought Clove along to keep you company. She'll make a fine travelin' companion, won't you, Cleo — won't you, Clove?"

Ethel, who was almost as pale as her white collar, put her hand to her throat.

"Traveling — traveling companion?" she faltered. "What do you mean? Where are you taking us? Oh, Nell, I'm so frightened!"

"You nice lady," came from the old woman, who was grinning widely. "You no get scared. Everyt'ing all right. You maybe go on a visit for a little while with me, and I show you pretty things. See!" and she held out her hand. Nell took from it a bracelet, apparently of finely wrought gold. Out of curiosity the girls examined it until they felt Richmond observing them strangely. With a shudder Nell handed it back. The moment the woman had it in her hand again Richmond seized it viciously.

"Tryin' to get away with somethin', hey?" he snarled. "We was to go fifty-fifty on all stuff you picked up, an' you know it. Where'd you get this, hey? Some fool lady who wanted her fortune told, I reckon."

The woman nodded, and grinned. Then she shrugged her shoulders and spread her hands wide — disdainfully.

"What would you? I must live. People say Clovita has the gift of prophecy. As to that —"

She was interrupted by the arrival of four men on ponies. They rode swiftly up, looked at the car and its occupants for a moment, then turned to Richmond.

"Good work," one of them said. "Yuh shore know yore doggies, Jack. We all set?"

"Yep. Hey, Clove, pile out. Here's where you get yore liver shook up good. Sheldon, slide off that war horse an' let a lady up. Come on, Cleo, shake yore stumps. When you get up there, hang on. Don't let 'er throw yuh. Ready? *Alley-oop!*"

With a groan, the old woman, assisted by Sheldon and Richmond, climbed to the back of the pony Sheldon had just quit. Once in the saddle, she took the reins with a practiced hand and settled her dresses about her with supreme confidence. Evidently she had been a rider in her day, but now she made a strange picture sitting proudly on the horse, her head thrown back, surveying with a scornful eye those on the ground.

Richmond grinned widely.

"Quite a gal," he said to Sheldon. "Feel O.K., Clove? That bronc's gentle, an' you won't have no trouble with her. If she rears, sock her on the head."

"Clovita know," the woman replied with dignity. "But I not hit a horse on the head — never. They die from that. Clovita rode horses before you were born. Wild horses, that ran like fire! No one could ride like Clovita, I —"

"Hang it up," Richmond said brutally. Then: "Miss Manley, I must ask you to change cars at this station. Sorry, but the road ain't so good fer autos. The other young gals too. Boys, pile off. We go back in the car. You girls ride with Clove. We'll see you later, so don't pine too much when we leave. And now — *adios*." He bowed mockingly.

"What do you mean?" Belle demanded, the blood coming to her cheeks like a flame. "You won't dare take us! We must go home immediately! If my father hears about this, you're life won't be worth a plugged nickel!" Unconsciously she had quoted Roy. "Dad'll kill you!"

Richmond looked at her, a grudging admiration in his eyes.

"Just take it easy, girlie," he said gently. "Nothin' is goin' to happen to you or your friends. You'll be as safe here as if you were home. This is just a little matter between yore father an' us, an' we take this way to settle it. See? But don't get fretful. We may be rustlers an' all that, but we're men. I just want to add one thing." His eyes narrowed.

"As long as you behave yourselves, you can do pretty much as you please an' nobody will touch you. But if you try to escape —" He took a heavy gun from his pocket and handed it up to Clovita as she sat on the pony. "Clovita," he continued sternly, "take a pot shot at that hunk of wood stickin' out by that rock."

The gun roared. Wide eyed, the girls looked to where Richmond pointed. The stick had disappeared.

"That white blaze on the tree over there."

Another roar. A tiny dot appeared in the center of the blaze.

"I guess you girls see she can shoot some. Clovita, you know what I told you. Let 'em ride ahead an' keep their distance. If they bolt, bring down the horse an' let 'em walk the rest of the way. If they start to run, just nip 'em a *leetle* bit. Then you won't have no more trouble. You know where to head for. We'll meet you there later."

He stopped and looked at the girls, who stood by the car, Belle defiant, Ethel frankly trembling, Nell pale, but game.

"I'm sorry to have to do this, but you'll understand why later," Richmond went on. "When we hear from yore dad an' if he answers the way we think he will, you'll be home right soon. If not —" He shrugged his shoulders. "But I'm not worrying about that. Now, climb aboard, you girls. I guess you all can ride. If not, you'll have to learn quick. The ponies are gentle an' won't buck none. Come on, boys." He entered the car. From behind the wheel he stuck his head out. "Clove," he called sharply, "remember what I told you! Don't let 'em get funny, or you'll wish you hadn't! Keep that gun out! Hop in here, you birds. We got to get this car back. Well, girls —" and he grinned and removed his hat — "see you later! So long! Have a nice trip!"

CHAPTER XVIII

BUG EYE SINGS

The small group of riders in that clearing in Thunder Canyon sat silent on ponies that pawed the ground restlessly. The old woman who stood before them, gun in hand, whistled shrilly. Out of the cabin bounded a dog, a huge mastiff.

"Kind of thinkin' things over now, ain't ye?" the woman cackled. "You fellers jest keep yer hands on the pommels of yer saddles — no lower. What's the idee, scarin' peaceful folks outen their sleep?"

"Well, ma'am," Gus drawled, "course we didn't know you was restin'. But it seems to me like we didn't have no band playin' when we rode up. An' if it's all the same to you, keep an easy finger on that trigger. She might be loaded, an' accidents will happen."

"You bet she's loaded! Heavy buckshot, too! Don't make no mistake about that! What you-all want?"

"Nothing, of you," Roy spoke up loudly. "We didn't even know you were here. We were riding up the canyon, and just happened on your place."

"Ye did, hey?" The woman considered this, but did not lower the rifle. "Don't sound likely. There's not many folks ride by here nowadays. What's yer business?"

"Sellin' seed catalogs," Nick answered.

"Seed catalogs? Ain't never heard mention of 'em. But let me tell you — this here canyon ain't healthy fer strangers, especially them that carry guns in saddle-holsters. If I was you, I'd turn right around and ride the other way. The scenery is fine at the other end."

"We're not looking at scenery," Teddy said shortly. "And we're anxious to get on. So if you'll just depress that cannon of yours, we'll be on our way."

"In a powerful hurry, ain't ye? Sol —" this to the dog — "jest you do a little investigatin'."

To the surprise of the boys, the dog walked forward, stiff legged, and sniffed loudly at the ponies and their riders. The horses watched him with suspicious eyes, but made no attempt to bolt. The inspection over, the dog returned to his mistress and casually flopped down at her feet. Then, and not till then, did the rifle butt rest upon the ground. The woman leaned on the barrel, her eyes glittering strangely.

"Lucky fer ye my dawg gives ye a clean bill," she said, with a little laugh. "Sol, here, is my outpost, an' nothin' goes by here that he don't give the once over — not nothin'!" She spat energetically. "Now, if you-all have a mind to, ye can ride on. But stay clear of the cabin. Sol don't like strangers."

Bug Eye cast a quick look at Teddy.

"Maybe we ain't in such a hurry as we was," he stated carelessly. "Kind of hot, ridin'." He dismounted slowly, and gave the reins of his mount to Gus to hold. "I guess you won't mind if I go around back an' help myself to a little water outen the pump, ma'am?"

"Hold up!"

The rifle barrel menaced the figure on foot. Bug Eye started in simulated surprise. "You're goin' to stay right where you air," the woman said viciously. "Don't you come snoopin' around me! Sol, watch him!" The dog trotted forward, teeth bared, growling menacingly. "Puncher, if you want to stay whole, don't move! My dawg ain't had a workout in two weeks, an' he sure craves action!"

Bug Eye looked down at the animal, thrust out his hand experimentally, and then quickly withdrew it.

"I ain't exactly aimin' to take on no dog," he muttered. "I guess you don't like visitors, ma'am, from the looks of things. Well, I stay thirsty, I can see that." Keeping an eye on the dog, he remounted. "You ain't never heard of the book of etiquette, I reckon. Ought to get it, ma'am. Do you a lot of good. It says in there to always treat a guest with the utmost consideration."

While he was talking, Bug Eye glanced rapidly toward the cabin. He gave an almost imperceptible jerk to his head, and the others gradually worked their horses a bit nearer the hut and in a wider circle. "You must be right lonely here, all alone. Got a radio? You ought to get one. Heard a new song on the radio only last night. Goes something like this:" He threw back his head, and raised his voice almost to a shout:

> "Come out o' the kitchen, Mary darlin',
> Come out o' the kitchen, Mary Ann.
> Come out —"

"Stop that yellin'!" the woman cried fiercely. "Stop it, I tell ye! If you don't —" She raised the gun, her face twisted into a snarl of rage.

"I'm stoppin'," Bug Eye said quickly. "I thought you might like to hear it. No need to get nasty. An' that gun makes me nervous. Snakes, you sure are touchy, ma'am! Objectin' to a little singin'!"

Once more his eyes roved in the direction of the cabin. The interior was dark and the windows gave no indication of what was within. Bug Eye waved his hand expressively, so that it would be visible to any one who might be watching.

"With all this canyon to fool around in, you oughtn't to be so touchy over a song," the puncher went on.

"Well, I am!" the woman snapped. "I don't like noise — especially that kind. I think you-all mentioned somethin' about ridin' on, a ways back. If I was you, I'd do jest that. Soon be dark, an' it ain't nice to be alone in the canyon at night," and the woman snickered.

"No, I reckon not," Gus drawled. He winked at Teddy. "Is there any place we could stop if we didn't make the end by night?"

"Don't know." The woman backed into the doorway and glanced swiftly behind her. Then she faced the riders again. "Good-bye. Don't come no closer as you go along. My finger ain't as steady as it once was, an' this gun might go off."

Roy whispered to the others:

"Come on, let's be going. We're wasting time here. She'd just as soon pepper us as not. I'd like to come by here later, when she isn't so lively."

Teddy chirped to Flash. Slowly the five riders filed past the cabin. Their last vision of the woman was as she stood in the doorway, her rifle held in the crook of her arm, her lips compressed tightly. As they turned their backs to her, each felt a prickly sensation run up his spine, as if those black eyes were boring into him.

When they rounded a bend, out of sight and hearing of the cabin, Roy called a halt.

"Well," he said, laughing shortly. "That's that! What a friendly customer *she* was! What the mischief do you suppose she was afraid of? I wonder —" His face flushed, as an idea came to him suddenly. "Do you suppose —"

"I was supposin' that all along," Bug Eye answered dryly. "The girls! It sure looked like a likely place to hide 'em. But they're not there — not now, anyways. I made sure of that. Unless they was tied up tight an' couldn't move," he added, his face serious.

"I kind of thought you had an idea behind that crazy song of yours," Teddy remarked. "And when you waved, too. But I couldn't see a thing through those windows. I'm afraid there's not much to it, Bug Eye. If I thought there was a possibility of Belle being hidden in there, I'd rush it, woman or no woman! But what's the use? We'd only get into trouble and maybe some one would have his head blown off. That was a powerful gun she had there. Besides, if the girls were there, there'd be men about to prevent any rescue or escape. What do you think about it, Roy?"

"I'm willing to admit I didn't get it at all," his brother answered. "But now you speak of it, there's nothing more likely than that the girls would be taken to some such place as that. Then with that old woman and all — you remember what Ike Natick said about the woman? There she was, as big as life, and then some. But I reckon it was another woman. That was a clever idea of yours, that song, Bug Eye. It proved one thing to me — that the girls are not there now, whether they will be later or not. Even if they were bound, they would have made some noise when they heard us. We came up too suddenly to allow that gunwoman any time to gag them. But it looks suspicious! As soon as we come into her yard, she's out with her rifle and tells us to make ourselves scarce. What for? She must have had some reason!"

Teddy shook his head, and Nick said:

"She's too many for me. But there's something in the wind besides the smell of fryin' onions, or I'm a ring-tailed dodo-bird. That hag'll bear watchin'. It ain't natural for a woman to be as suspicious as she was without havin' something on her mind, an' I'd give a lot to know what it is. I'll bet if we knew, we wouldn't have so far to go to find Belle Ada and the others! But —" He shrugged his shoulders expressively. "You can't go over an' threaten to shoot her unless she tells all she knows. It ain't bein' done this season."

"Nope, boys, we got to ride on to the caves. Maybe when we get there we can discover somethin' to go by. This Ike Natick — he's with our outfit, you know — strikes me as a level-headed cow puncher. Besides that, there ain't no ribbons tied on him, he's all man. When he says a thing, I listens. An' he said he's got a hunch the rustlers headed for Sholo Caves. That's enough fer me. What do ya say, Roy — do we go?"

"We do, Bug Eye. Dad might be waiting for us when we get near Gravestone Falls. I hope so, anyway. Hit it up, boys, it's getting dark."

Once more the riders, single file, made their way up the canyon. The sun threw its slanting rays on the brown stone walls, streaking them with gold. Below them the stream gurgled over the rocks. Back of them, in a small clearing an old woman stood in the doorway of a cabin, leaning on the barrel of a rifle, her eyes fixed toward them in a malevolent glare.

CHAPTER XIX

INTO THE CAVE

The rocky walls of the gorge echoed to the sound of the slow, deliberate hoof-beats as four horses were urged over the trail on the edge of Thunder Canyon, the steeds carrying three girls followed by an old woman.

Two days later this same trail was to be the path of another group of riders, who, doggedly pursuing, were to find this same deep gulch the scene of a desperate fight for the rescue of these present travelers.

Slowly they went, those ahead riding unwillingly. In the extreme rear rode the woman, a striking counterpart to another of her sex who dwelt in a lonely cabin on the edge of a clearing, long since passed by the wayfarers.

They had halted for a moment at this hut, and their guard, who carried before her a heavy gun held in a firm hand, had whistled to the cabin's occupant. When the second woman appeared Belle started, as did the others, at the remarkable resemblance between the two. They were exactly of the same height and their faces were strangely similar, as though the lines in each countenance had come of the same experiences. "Sisters — maybe twins," Nell had whispered, and the others nodded.

For a few minutes the two old hags remained in close conversation, the one who had come with the girls never for a second relaxing her vigilance or allowing the gun to point in any direction but toward the horses. With that blue barrel menacing them, the girls knew that escape was out of the question. They seemed in no present danger, however, and Ethel had largely recovered from her first fright. Belle, tight-lipped, was occupied with furious thoughts.

That such a thing could happen in a civilized country! They were kidnapped — neither more nor less! Kidnapped! Belle bit her lips and her face clouded. Mother! How she would worry when she found out! They *must* escape somehow, and get back home before her mother heard they were missing!

It was characteristic of the girl that she gave her own safety scarcely a thought. Richmond had said they were not to be harmed, but that they were to be held until her father did the rustler's bidding. Belle smarted at the indignity of being a weapon in the hands of the horse thieves, for she now realized who her captors were.

Of course she had heard of the note her father had received, and gradually the conviction had grown on her that this was the means the rustlers had taken to "square up" matters between them and the X Bar X. The cowards! To use girls to effect their revenge! Belle's lips curled in contempt. If that was the kind they were, they couldn't stand up long against the punchers on the X Bar X! Why, Teddy and Roy would soon send them running for cover.

As the girl thought of her brothers, her heart beat rapidly with hope. They would hear of their disappearance and ride after them. If they only knew which way to head! All sorts of wild ideas surged through the girl's brain, but she realized that it would be impossible to send word to the ranch. All they could do was to wait and pray that the boys started in the right direction, when they took up the chase.

All this time the two women were talking. Now and then their guard would nod in the girls' direction and the other woman would grin evilly. Of the two, Belle much preferred the one who was riding with them. Somehow, she seemed more kind, even though, thus far, she had treated them with small consideration. Still, Belle felt that she would do nothing cruel as long as they made no attempt to escape.

At last the conversation was concluded and Clovita returned to her horse. After several attempts, and with much grunting, she succeeded in regaining the saddle, her sister, if such the other women were, watching her amusedly, making no offer of assistance. Then, with the gun pointing at their backs, the girls continued their weary ride.

Nell made several efforts at finding out their destination, but each question was received in stony silence. At length she desisted, and the girls talked in low tones among themselves. As they rode on, their courage returned to them, and even Ethel seemed brighter. Belle Ada comforted her with the declaration that Teddy and Roy and her father and Peter Ball would soon be aware of their capture — she preferred that word to kidnapping — and would ride in search of them. With both ranches, the X Bar X and 8 X 8, in pursuit, their rescue was but a matter of time. But even while she was speaking, Belle realized how slim was the chance of any one finding them in this wilderness, and her heart sank within her.

Mile after mile along the canyon the girls, followed closely by their guard, rode in silence. As night approached and they still went on, Belle saw Ethel's shoulders shake with dry sobs. The woman in the rear gave no sign, but Belle rode to her friend and, reaching out, seized her hand.

"Don't give in, Ethel dear," Belle whispered. "Look at Nell! She's taking it like a veteran. After all this is over and the boys are with us again and those rustlers are back in jail, think of the experiences we'll have had. Why, when you go back to New York and tell people that you've been captured by a bunch of real outlaws and made to ride for miles along a canyon, to — to —"

91

"That's just it," Ethel replied. "Where are we going? Where is she taking us? I'm so frightened!"

"What, you frightened?" Nell scoffed, although her own voice was none too strong. "How about that time you and I were out sailing on Long Island Sound by Fire Island and the storm came up? You weren't scared then, Ethel. And that was *lots* worse than this is! Why, I think this is sort of fun! As Belle says, Teddy and Roy will find us, and I guess we can take care of ourselves. Come on, Ethel, don't let that horrid old woman see that Easterners aren't as brave as Westerners! Buck up!"

"That's the talk!" Belle exclaimed, giving Ethel's hand a squeeze of encouragement. "Here —" She passed Ethel a tiny handkerchief, seemingly inadequate, but with a smile Ethel dabbed at her eyes and handed it back.

"I'm all right — now," she declared, patting the pony she was riding. "Belle, did you notice this horse? Isn't he a positive beauty? I wish I owned him!"

"Something tells me you will, later," Belle answered giving a laugh. Ethel's smile had cheered her immensely and things seemed not nearly so dark. After all, this certainly was a unique experience.

Belle thought of the Western books she had read and how she had scoffed at the adventures the heroes and heroines had gone through.

"As though we of the West lived in a land of nothing but rattlesnakes, cyclones, and rustlers!" she once exclaimed. "Those things they write about just don't happen!"

And now here she was, riding through a canyon to some unknown, far-off place, with a savage old woman forcing them on with a pistol!

"I guess they do happen, after all," she said to herself ruefully. "Although I'd rather read about this than be where I am!"

She was wise enough, however, to keep her fears from the other girls. Indeed, she did all in her power to cheer them, and insisted that they would be rescued as soon as the boys and her father and Mr. Ball found that they were missing.

"And that'll be as soon as Mrs. Ball telephones home to see that we arrived safely," she added. Had she known at the time that two whole days were to elapse before the kidnapping was discovered, her courage might not have been quite so high. Perhaps it was fortunate that she remained in ignorance of this fact.

They were nearing the end of the canyon now, and Belle looked sharply about her. Here the cut seemed deeper than at any other place and the trail narrower, as though Nature wanted to end this scene with a setting of more than usual grandeur. The canyon walls fell straight away, ending at the gurgling stream far below them, and on either side the mountains arose, forming a protection from any storm which might try to invade this fastness.

Belle, gazing for a moment down into the tremendous depths, shivered in spite of herself. A misstep here would mean quick, sure death.

Now the path dipped sharply for a short space, and, when they reached a level spot once more, the woman with the gun called:

"You stop here. Get off ponies."

Wonderingly, the girls obeyed, noticing that the woman herself stayed mounted.

"Go ahead. Leave ponies," was the next command. As the girls proceeded, their guard kept a careful eye on them. Not for a moment did the gun relax from its threat.

Before they had gone fifty feet Belle and the others saw the reason they were told to dismount. Ahead of them, hewn in the solid rock, was an entrance to a cavern of some sort. Behind its rough, wooden door it was intensely dark, and the girls caught themselves thinking that if they were compelled to enter this cave they might never see the light of day again. But as they approached they saw that the entrance led to a wide, airy room of rock, beyond which a light of some sort glowed. This light was not visible from the outside.

Now the woman slid from her horse and walked toward the girls.

"You go in," she said shortly, motioning with the gun barrel.

"In there?" Ethel gasped, her face pale.

The woman nodded firmly, then bent to explain:

"You no worry. I here. I no hurt you nor let any one else hurt you. I not a bad woman, but —" She seemed about to say more, then closed her lips tightly. Once more she indicated the mouth of the cave.

The girls had no choice. With fear in their hearts and with faltering steps, they entered.

CHAPTER XX

AN ATTEMPT THAT FAILED

Once within the cave, Belle took a deep breath. Nothing had happened yet. They were still alive, at all events. She led the way toward the light they had seen, and, to her amazement, she discovered that on the left a passageway led to another cavern, larger than the first, which also was illuminated.

Hearing a shuffling step behind them, the girls turned swiftly, but it was only the old woman, the light from the lamp in the wall shining on the metal of her leveled revolver. Whatever else might be said for her, she allowed her charges no chance to escape.

"Ahead," she grunted, and slowly the girls entered the second cave. This had a high, rocky roof. Several lighted lamps were fastened to the walls. There was furniture of a sort, there being a heavy table in the center, while arranged along the wall were makeshift cots, five of them.

With a slight gasp, Ethel leaned against the table. The woman grinned.

"No get scared," she said. "All right. You safe in here. We wait now till men come. But you no worry. I here. You all safe."

"That isn't much assurance," Nell whispered to Belle. "What a strange place! Surely they can't mean to keep us here! Ethel will almost die of fright."

She cast a swift look at her cousin, but the girl seemed more courageous than she had been, probably realizing that nothing could be gained by showing her fear. So, although her underlip trembled pitifully, Ethel suddenly approached their guard.

"Do you think we're going to submit to this?" she demanded, a high color in her cheeks. "That you — an old woman — can keep us here? Don't think we're afraid of you! We could — What's that?" she broke off suddenly, pointing to the doorway.

Unsuspectingly, the woman turned. The next moment Ethel's two hands had closed over the gun, and, with a fierce look of determination in her eyes, she struggled fiercely. In a flash the other two leaped to her assistance, and the woman was disarmed. Ethel, the one who had been most frightened, had done what the others dared not do!

"Now," she panted, trembling so that she could scarcely stand, "the tables are turned! Let us out of here!"

The woman shrugged her shoulders stolidly, and stood to one side.

94

"Where you go?" she muttered. "Horses gone. They go by themselves where you no find them. You want to walk, all right. Long ways," and she grinned.

Ethel threw the gun on the table in despair.

"We could never make it," she stammered, her breath choked in her throat. "It's too far! This horrible canyon —" she could not finish.

"Where are the horses?" Bell asked, stepping forward.

Once more Clovita shrugged her shoulders, spreading her hands wide.

"You look," she said indifferently. "You no find. They far away. Besides —" she stopped, holding her hand to her ear — "I hear men coming," she concluded, with another grin.

"The rustlers!" Nell gasped, seizing Belle's arm. "They're coming here!"

A clatter of horses' feet sounded on the path outside. There were some muttered sentences, which the girls could not catch, and a figure filled the doorway. It was Richmond, the man who had driven the car.

"Evenin' ladies," he greeted them, smiling sardonically, his hat sweeping the ground. Another smile was on his face as he turned to the men behind him. "Our guests," he added, and the girls detected a sarcastic note.

Belle recognized the four men who had met them at the entrance to the canyon, but this time there were two others with them. One of them looked vaguely familiar, but Belle could not remember where she had seen him before.

Ethel shrank against the wall.

"Don't be scared — we're not poison," Richmond sneered. "Though your dad seems to think we are," he added, looking at Belle Ada. "I see you got here all right," he said to Clovita.

The woman nodded, but made no answer. She glared at Richmond from beneath beetled brows, her head bent low. Belle, observing this by-play, was at a loss to account for the woman's apparent antagonistic attitude toward Richmond until she recalled the episode at the canyon's mouth, when Clovita had protested at the garbling of her name. Yet it did not seem reasonable that any one would hate a man simply because he had called her by a name not her own.

Richmond motioned Clovita to him, and for some moments the two remained in low-voiced conversation. Then Richmond spoke to the girls:

"We have to leave now, sorry as you are to see us go," he said, grinning. "But remember this — two of us will be on guard all night at the door of this cave. If any of you try to get out —" his eyes glittered dangerously — "you'll wish you hadn't, that's all. Clove, here, will get you anything you want in the line of food. She knows where the grub an' water is. As for beds —" he motioned toward the rude cots. "This ain't no hotel, an'

95

you'll have to make out the best you can. The sooner yore dad comes through, the sooner you'll be out of here. We'll send him a note to-morrow or the next day — give him a little time to think it over first. In the meanwhile, as long as you girls behave, you'll be safe. If you don't — well, that's up to you. Come on, boys — we vamose. *Adios, señoritas! Hasta mañana!*"

He was gone. The old woman walked slowly over to the table and casually picked up the gun Ethel had thrown there. She carried it to one of the couches and tossed it down as though it was of no consequence. Then, shuffling across the cave, she disappeared into the other room.

The three girls, with heavy hearts, watched her depart. Escape seemed impossible, and even rescue appeared unthinkable in this dismal cave. Ethel struggled hard against tears, and succeeded for a time in holding them back. Belle and Nell themselves were not far from weeping. Outside, the sun was casting its last rays on the walls of the canyon, but those within the cavern knew nothing of this. They were held in a rocky jail, and guarding them were two outlaws who would not hesitate to shoot if the prisoners tried to escape. Small wonder that hope departed from them and for the first time they clung together, at length finding relief in the tears which had been for so long repressed.

Until far in the night the three girls sat on one of the cots, huddled close. The supper they had been given was coarse, but there was plenty of it. Yet they could not have eaten much had the meal been a royal banquet. It is impossible to feast when a lump keeps coming into one's throat and tears to the eyes.

But as time went on, and they still remained unmolested, they took heart again and conversed more cheerfully. True, it was lonesome and cold in the cave. But to-morrow, surely, help would come. To-morrow — that seemed so far away, looking now into the blackness of the cave. Even the friendly stars were hidden from them!

But morning came at last, and with it hope. Clovita, who had slept near them, greeted them with a toothless smile and informed them that breakfast would soon be ready. With shudders, they disclaimed any desire to eat, but when they saw the food before them their appetites conquered and they fell to with a will. About two hours after sunrise Richmond appeared and suggested they "come out an' get a breath of fresh air."

Realizing that they must preserve their strength, the girls walked slowly to the mouth of the cave. The canyon was drenched with the morning sun, and it seemed impossible that any villainy could exist amid such pleasant surroundings. Belle caught Richmond watching her with an amused smile on his lips, as though he read her thoughts, and she turned her back on him coolly.

"As you please," he said shortly, as he walked toward one of his companions. "Like it or not — you stay here until we hear from yore dad. We send the note to-morrow, askin' fer a certain amount of money. And if you're wise, you'll hope he sends it, *pronto*! We've got to get paid for the time we spent in jail, due to your respected parent's activities," and he grinned again sardonically.

"You'll not get dad to send you any money!" Belle exclaimed hotly. "The only thing he'll send you will be hot lead!"

For a moment Richmond looked at her, then he laughed.

"What d'you think of little Miss Spitfire?" he asked his companions. "I'll be sort of sorry to see her leave, I'm gettin' so used to her!" Then, changing his tone, he added:

"As far as slingin' lead goes, we got two men who are experts in that line. They come from — well, not from around here, at any rate. An' if yore old man wants to try a little gun play, we're all set. In fact, anxious! I ain't forgot the fact that he rode all the way over to Hawley just to see that we got ours. Nor we ain't forgot — some other things, too. So let him come on." His eyes narrowed. "But if he knows what's good for him, he'll bring an army when he arrives, 'cause if we start shootin', it ain't goin' to be safe fer himself nor fer them two brothers of yours, either!"

Turning on his heel, he walked up the trail, his heavy colt swinging at his side. Belle felt a shudder pass over her.

How much longer were they to be kept in the lonesome place with only a fierce old woman as a companion? How long?

CHAPTER XXI

THE RECKLESS RIDER

Dusk had settled over Thunder Canyon. A cool breeze blew down from the mountains, and the five horses sniffed it gratefully. They had carried their riders far that day, over a trail which stiffened their leg muscles and dulled their eyes, from demanding constant attention to its treacherous unevenness. But they had done their work well, and now they were near the end of their journey.

Teddy, who was riding ahead, turned in the saddle.

"How much further?" he asked of Nick.

"Not much. You've kind of forgot this path, ain't yuh? Well, it's a long time since I been over it myself, but I'm thinkin' Gravestone Falls is just ahead. Right, Gus?"

"I reckon," Gus drawled. "She's narrowin' down closer, anyhow," and he jerked his head toward the other side, which, it seemed to the riders, had been gradually coming nearer as they loped along.

But a scant hour of daylight remained, and Roy, realizing they had small chance to join his father and the others, once full darkness had descended, urged Teddy to set a faster pace. The tired horses responded willingly, and the men made better time toward their objective.

For the last hour or so the boys' thoughts had been taken up with the strange old woman they had encountered in the clearing. Certainly she fitted Ike Natick's description of the woman whom he had seen in the car which had borne the three girls from the 8 X 8. Could it be that the outlaws had forced their prisoners to remain in that hut over Saturday and Sunday, then, this morning, had taken them farther on, so as to be safer from pursuit?

Teddy, revolving the subject over in his mind, thought it extremely likely. If only they had discovered on Saturday that the girls had been taken, they might have had them at home by this time! Teddy remembered, with an ironical laugh, that he and Roy had at first planned to visit the 8 X 8 on the very day the girls were kidnapped.

Then the storm had come, and they had postponed their journey until this morning, when it was too late! What had happened to Belle Ada — and the others — during those two days when he and Roy were hanging around the ranch, talking over ways to prevent the rustlers from executing their threat? Why, at the very moment when Mr. Manley and the two boys had been deciding what part of the range to watch, the outlaws had acted and had taken revenge!

Teddy grew stiff and his hands clenched. All because of a storm! If it hadn't rained, he and Roy could have been after the rustlers almost as soon as they got started. Or they might even have arrived at the 8 X 8 at the same time that the puncher, Richmond, had come with the false note.

Teddy shook his head helplessly and gazed ahead through the gathering dusk. To his ears came the sound of falling water, but the boy could not tell whether it was Gravestone Falls or merely the brook below growing more turbulent.

"Here's hoping we meet dad soon," Roy declared, peering across the canyon. "It'll be night before long, and we'll have a pretty hard job of finding him then."

Teddy agreed, with a nod.

"He'll be there. Remember, we were delayed by that gunwoman in the cabin. If dad rode straight on, which I think he did, he's probably at the falls now. Nick, watch your step! There's a mean bit of trail right here."

Nick, who was following Roy, grunted to show that he understood, and cautioned Gus and Bug Eye, who drew up in the rear. Then he called to Teddy:

"Expect to run across yore friend who rides sidesaddle, Ted?"

"Sidesaddle? Oh, you mean the puncher who slouches to the left? I sure do, Nick! I hope to, anyhow. I guess Roy does, also. We'll ask him for his card and where he got 'Reltsur' for a name."

"You think Richmond and Reltsur are the same man?"

"Yep! Nothing else but! The handwriting on the note that Mrs. Ball showed us and on the note that dad got are identical. We noticed particularly the capital R; didn't we, Roy? Alike as two peas. I'm sure counting on meeting that waddy personally, Nick!"

"Wish you luck." Nick rested his hand on the gun which hung from a saddle-holster. "But don't hog the action, Teddy — don't hog it! Me an' Gus an' Bug Eye are just rustin' away from peacefulness. When the music starts, Teddy, we'll be there! Oh, we'll be there!"

"I'll tell a maverick!" Roy exclaimed. "We all will, Nick! And if those dirty horse thieves have harmed Belle, or even frightened her, we'll —"

"Take it easy, boy," Gus drawled, laying his hand on Roy's shoulder for a moment. "Belle can take care of herself, and of the two that's with her, if she has to. I know Belle! Not like you do, of course, but enough to say that she's one game little lady and that she can hold her own with any sneak-thief that ever ran from a jack-rabbit. Now don't you start worryin', you nor Teddy either. So far, yore takin' it standin' up. Keep it up, boys; it won't be long now!

99

"To-morrow we can head fer Sholo Caves, and then, if Ike is right, we'll have all three girls safe an' sound. Then we can settle our accounts with Reltsur an' his gang." He paused for a moment, then went on:

"I know I'm talkin' like a Dutch Uncle, but I want you to know how I feel, an' how Nick an' the rest of us feel, too. I'm not sayin' what we'd do to get Belle back. I guess you know, right enough."

Roy turned and looked at his friend, silently grasped the hand that was held out to him, and then grinned.

"You win, Gus. No more grousing. Star, get along there! We rest soon. Guess a good drink from that old stream will feel mighty fine, hey? Well, you'll get it. Come along, now. There's a lot of green grass waiting for you."

Suddenly, from the depths of the canyon, came a long shrill howl. The horses, hearing it, snorted in fear. The grin froze on Roy's face.

"Timber wolf," he said shortly. "A brute, from its yell. Didn't know they came down this far."

Teddy frowned fiercely, and, unconsciously, his hand sought his gun butt. There were wolves in this canyon. Belle, Ethel and Nell were somewhere up that long, winding trail. Wolves! The boy's hand tightened on the gun. No, he would not, could not, think that!

Now the men rode along in silence. The scream of that animal had set their nerves on edge, and they were in no mood for conversation. It would have gone ill for the outlaws had the rescue riders encountered them at that moment. Each man gazed straight ahead, his body rigid in the saddle. Each pony felt the hand holding the reins stiffen and tighten ever so slightly. Putting their heads down, the ponies plodded on and on.

Now the noise of the falls could be heard distinctly. Teddy was about to make a remark when he caught himself up quickly and motioned for silence. Wondering, those following came to a halt and listened. Then they understood.

Above the distant roar of Gravestone Falls came another sound, a staccato drumming, which, to the trained ear, was unmistakable. With a quick movement the riders leaped their horses off the path and into the brush. There they waited, listening to those approaching hoof-beats. Nearer and nearer they came. Suddenly Teddy leaned over and tapped Roy.

Around a bend in the trail came a horseman. He was riding furiously, seemingly heedless of the desperate chance he was taking of being hurled to the rocks below. And as the boys watched, they saw something that caused their hearts to leap with a sudden fierce joy.

The horseman did not ride straight up in the saddle, but slouched to the left!

CHAPTER XXII

RETRIBUTION

Teddy's eyes flashed and he drew his revolver. He made as if to urge Flash out into the trail to face the oncoming horseman, but Roy laid a restraining hand on his arm.

"Wait!" he cautioned tensely. "Not yet!"

Now the rider was nearly opposite those hidden in the brush. Roy looked at Teddy and Nick, then nodded. Carelessly the five men walked their horses into the middle of the trail, adequately covering it. The slouched horseman yelled, pulled back sharply on the reins, and brought his pony to a sudden, sliding halt.

"You crazy fools!" he shouted. "Want to send me over the cliff? What in time's the matter with you-all, jumpin' out on me like that?"

"Well, now, mister, we weren't aimin' to do just that," Gus drawled mildly. "But we heard you comin', an' we kind o' thought you might like to palaver a little."

"Well, I don't!" The man turned angrily toward Gus. "An' I'll thank you to move aside an' let me by! I'm in a hurry!"

"Shorely you can't be in a hurry on a nice evenin' like this!" Nick suggested gently. "Seems like yuh ought to be ridin' along slow like, observin' the birds an' the flowers, an' maybe tossin' sticks with paper tied to 'em down into the gully. Hey?"

"Stand aside, you locoed cow-nurse! I ain't got no time fer no foolishness! Once more, I'm tellin' yuh —"

Teddy saw the man's hand go for his gun. Quick as a flash, the boy drew and the reckless horseman found himself looking into the muzzle of a blue-barreled Colt. With his hand on his belt, the man hesitated, then gave a sneering laugh.

"Kind o' sudden, ain't yuh? Well, suppose you speak up an' tell me what this is all about. I come along this here trail, aimin' to make the canyon's end before ten to-night, when a gang of stick-up artists shoves a six-gun down my throat! If it's money you want —" The man reached in his shirt pocket and drew out some silver, which he threw contemptuously on the ground at Flash's feet. "Here! That's all I got. Pretty poor pickin', hey, boys?"

"Pretty considerable of a fool, you are," drawled Gus contemptuously.

Teddy's eyes narrowed.

"Take it easy," he said in a voice that, somehow, reminded Nick of a taut violin string. "You know we're not highwaymen. We want to ask you some questions — *Reltsur.*"

The man started, almost imperceptibly, then recovered his composure.

"Well, I ain't no encyclopedia of information, but I'll do the best I can," he replied sarcastically. "Only hurry up. It's gettin' late."

Teddy made a motion with his head, and Bug Eye moved toward the rider. He reached over and quickly yanked the man's gun from its holster.

"Playin' safe, hey? Afraid I'll pull on yuh with that starin' me in the face?" and he nodded at the gun Teddy held.

"Never mind that," Roy said sharply. "We'll do the asking, and you the answering. First, where's the rest of your gang?"

"Gang?" The man laughed shortly. "Don't know what yuh mean. I ain't got no gang. I'm just a poor little me — all alone," and he laughed again.

"And I suppose you don't know where Sholo Caves are?" Teddy asked, watching him closely through the dusk.

"Sholo — Sholo Caves?" This time there was no mistaking the start. "Why — I heard tell of 'em. Back a ways, ain't they?"

"Maybe!" Teddy rode closer. Suddenly he jammed the gun into the man's ribs, causing a grunt of pain and surprise. "Now answer this, and answer it quick!" he snapped. "Where are Belle Manley and her two friends?"

For a moment the man seemed too stunned to speak.

"Belle — Manley?" he faltered. "I — I don't know what you're talkin' about. How should I know? Who are they? What —"

"Save it!" Teddy's voice cut the air like a knife. "Once more — where is my sister?" The hammer of the gun came back with an ominous click. Wide-eyed with fright, the man stared into the piercing eyes before him. Then he gulped.

"Yuh — yuh got me cold!" he whispered. "I'm sunk! I'll tell — I'll tell everything!"

Suddenly, with a wild yell, he sank his spurs deep into the pony's side. The horse, frantic with pain, leaped forward, striking Roy's mount head on and then swerved to the fiercely pulled reins.

"Get him!" Gus yelled. "Nick, bust him wide open! Let him have it!"

Not a sound came from Teddy. Deliberately he raised his gun. There was a roar that echoed amid the canyon's walls, proving its name, and the fleeing rider crumpled in the saddle. The next moment he slid to the ground, and the horse, free of its burden, dashed along the trail, to disappear around the bend.

Teddy quickly dismounted.

"I hated to do it, but I had to," he said sadly. "You boys know I had to. I hope I didn't —"

He bent over the form on the ground. As he touched the man's arm a savage cry arose, and the figure came to life with a suddenness that sent Teddy staggering back, a dark stain on the boy's face showing where the closed fist had struck.

"He's all right," Teddy said shortly, wiping the blood from his cheek. "Sit up, you! Another break and I'll shoot off your head instead of your arm! Sit up now!"

Muttering under his breath, the man obeyed. He swayed where he sat, cuddling his arm, a look of anguish on his face. But the boys were in no mood for sympathy. There was other business on hand — business that must be transacted quickly.

"Going to answer the question?" Roy demanded, leaning over his horse and gazing at the form on the path.

"What question?" the man groaned.

"Where are those girls you brought from the 8 X 8?"

"I tell yuh I —" The grim Colt menaced his head, and the man shrank back. "Gimme time! I'm tryin' to tell yuh, ain't I! They're in —"

The boys listened eagerly, their hearts thumping madly. They leaned forward, Teddy kneeling on the ground, his eyes boring into those of the wounded man.

"They're — in — Sholo Caves!"

Then, with a sigh, the outlaw toppled over, his head hitting the ground with a thud, and he lay still.

CHAPTER XXIII

ON TO THE RESCUE

"Fainted," Bug Eye remarked, and leaped from his horse. Pulling his canteen from his saddle, he doused the man's face with the water in it, desisting at the first sign of returning consciousness. Replacing the top on the canteen, Bug Eye flung it down beside the silent figure and remounted.

"You-all heard what he said?" Nick asked excitedly. "Ike Natick was right! Sholo Caves! Come on, boys! Let that snake lie. He'll be all right with the water. We'll get him later. He's too badly shot up to move an' his horse is gone. Yow! We're off!"

With the news that they were on the right trail, came bounding hope and a joy that expressed itself in vigorous denunciation of Reltsur and his gang. With scarcely a backward glance, the five rode swiftly up the trail toward the falls that roared in the distance. They were not callous, but something more important than wounded outlaws sent them rushing forward.

"If we can only find dad!" Teddy yelled, as he guided Flash with a sure hand. "This blame darkness! We shan't be able to see a thing in a few minutes!"

"Can't help it," Roy answered. "If we don't meet dad, we'll go on ourselves. Guess we can handle any bunch of kidnappers that rides. How about it, boys?"

"You said a mouthful!" Gus roared. "Let 'em come shootin'! The more the merrier! We'll smoke 'em out, if we have to! No — guess we can't do that, on account of the girls. But we'll sure send some hot lead buzzin' 'round their ears!"

The full darkness of the canyon night came upon them as they rode, and, of necessity, they had to dismount and lead the ponies. Teddy fretted at the delay, but it was unavoidable, and they hurried as fast as was compatible with safety — and perhaps a little faster.

They soon reached Gravestone Falls, and all knew that the other side of the canyon was not two hundred yards across. To reach the caves, they had to turn sharply to the right and double back slightly on their trail. Had they known it, they could have come a much shorter way, as had the girls and their guard, who did not ride near the falls. But since they had arranged to meet Mr. Manley here, it was necessary that they take the longer route, even had they known of the shorter. At this point the canyon curved, the walls coming closer together, until, a short distance below the caves, they met.

The falls proper were not a part of the canyon itself, but, nevertheless, being near it, they fed the stream at its bottom. The roaring, while not tremendous, was loud enough to prevent any one on the other side of the canyon from hearing a call, however loud.

Teddy waited until the others were around him, then declared:

"I reckon we shan't find dad to-night! He may be across there, and he may not. Shouting won't do a bit of good. And we can't shoot — the rustlers might hear us and take alarm. Boys, it's up to us. Do we go on?"

"We do!" Roy exclaimed. "And not in the dark, either! Look!"

He pointed to the sky. Over the rim of the mountain a dull red crescent arose — the first of the full moon.

As the orb turned gradually from ruby to silver white, flooding the canyon with its glow, the five looked to their firearms. Then they slowly made their way along the rocky path. They had remounted again, knowing the ponies could see their way by the light of the moon, and, as they rounded the curve, following the gorge, the noise of the falls increased, then faded to a sullen murmur. They had left the meeting place behind, and with grim resolves to prove the caves could be taken by five determined men, all riding together, they urged their horses forward.

They remembered what Pop Burns had told them — that the caves were practically inaccessible unless attacked from both sides of the canyon at once. Yet this did not deter them. Their hearts high with hope, they felt capable of conquering any stronghold, no matter how well fortified. The girls were there — not half an hour's ride away! Could they stop now, with success almost in their grasp?

"Either we bring Belle out of here or we stay in ourselves," Roy whispered, as though to himself. But Teddy heard him, and nodded silently. They would fight — they would die — but they would not be beaten back!

"Almost there," Nick said in a low voice. "Let's stick together, boys. We can't afford to get separated. Roy, suppose you take charge."

"Right. Now let's see. Who knows anything about the layout of those caves?"

"I know they set pretty near the edge of the gully, Roy," Nick answered, in a doubtful voice. "An' I think you can come at them from either end. But *we* can't, 'cause the only way to get to the other side from where we are, is past them. So we'll have to depend on surprising that gang of rustlers before they know what's up. Once they discover us, we'll have to move fast."

Roy thought for a moment.

"If we only had a few more men! But we haven't, so what's the use of wishing? Teddy, some one suggested, a way back, that we send a man on ahead to investigate. What do you think about it?"

"Not much, Roy. If you want me to, I'll do it; but I can't see that we'd gain much. They've got a guard out — maybe two. I'm pretty sure of that. What we ought to do is to get up on them as quietly as we can, knock the guard off cold, if we have to, then depend on our guns for the rest." As he spoke the boy's eyes flashed and he breathed faster. When the time for action came he would be ready to do his part.

"Sounds good to me," Gus drawled. "Roy, when we start, we got to shoot as we go. I heard the bunch has two New York gunmen along. Well, we'll see how they like a taste of Western methods," and he smiled grimly.

"Then it's settled?" Roy asked, looking from one to the other. "We ride on together. When we get near, we slide off the broncs and nab the lookout, if there is one. Then — what's in our way we take out! I don't know how many men they've got, but unless it's an army we'll go through 'em. All set, boys?"

"All set!"

The answer came in tense whispers from men who were ready to face death — and expected to. Guns were loosened in holsters. Belts were tightened. Rifles were moved toward the rear of saddles to allow a quick descent from the pony. Long-barreled guns were useless in a hand to hand fight, and the boys put their faith in their automatic pistols.

As they started on this last leg of their journey toward an end none could foretell, each rider felt a great relief surge through him. The time had come. Ahead of them lay Sholo Caves, and within them the three girls were captives. They must be rescued. If some of the boys lost their lives — well, at least they could take some in payment. No matter what happened, they would go on to the end. Their task lay before them.

CHAPTER XXIV

OUT OF BONDAGE

Long, grey shadows flattened themselves against the walls of the canyon — moving shadows — five of them. The moonlight, except where it was cut off by the figures on horseback, flooded the rocky gorge.

The men were almost as silent as these silhouettes while they rode forward. The ponies, sensing the tenseness in the air, restrained their tendency to whinny at the ghostly trees along the sides.

After a short ride, Roy, who was leading, slid noiselessly from his bronco and waited on foot for the others, who, when they saw the boy dismount, did likewise.

"We'd better picket the ponies here," Roy whispered. "The ledge is plenty broad, and we may not find another place like this."

Without comment, the men obeyed. Then, slowly and cautiously, they crept forward, Roy and Teddy going first, followed by Nick, Gus, and Bug Eye. Suddenly a man's voice cut the silence. It came from behind a rock, not five feet from the ranchers.

"Makin' us lose our beauty sleep like this," the voice grumbled. "An' for what? Just 'cause that fool took it into his head to get the note to old man Manley to-night! As if to-morrow wouldn't do as well!"

"Yea, an' we got to stand guard over a passel o' senseless gals!" growled another. "Crazy, I calls it — plumb crazy! Why, the way old Reltsur, as he calls himself — wonder what his real name is? — the way he started with that note fer the X Bar X you'd think he was goin' to a fire! Lickety-cut, down the trail like a locoed steer. An' sometimes I think he is locoed, too — takin' to kidnappin' girls! Why, blame it all, they're more trouble than they're worth. Me, I told him that! But no, he would have his way. Fer revenge, he said. Huh! Revenge! What's he want revenge fer? Couple of hundred head of white-face Durhams 'ud be more to my notion. Got a match, Bill? This pipe's gone out. Guess she don't draw well."

Around the corner of the rock came the reflection of a tiny flame, and Teddy nudged Roy.

"Jump 'em?" he breathed. It was a tense question.

Roy shook his head. "Not yet. We may hear something that'll help us. Listen —"

The one who spoke first continued:

"He's a funny bird, that Reltsur. Now where'd he pick up a name like that? Sounds like a Russian dressing. You know, before we got mixed up with that X Bar X outfit he was O. K. Just a regular rustler then, an' he knew his stuff, let me tell yuh. Almost as good as that other waddy we had, who got knifed by Froud. What was his name, now? Well, don't matter. As I was sayin', this Reltsur was all right up to then. When we got nabbed at the fence he tried to slide out from under, but he gits his right under the left ear. Ever notice how funny he rides — leanin' to the left, kind of?"

"Yea, but he don't ride on his ear, does he?" the other chuckled. "Anyway, we got to give him credit fer arrangin' that little affair at Hawley. He sure turned that out proper. But what 'ud he want to go an' cart along those billies from New York fer? They ain't no good. They can't even shoot, though they said they could. Know where they are now? Back in town, playin' poker with the rest of our outfit. That's where we ought to be, 'stead of standin' here catchin' cold! What say we duck? Hey?"

Teddy seized Roy's arm. These two must be alone! What a chance! But now the other spoke again:

"Better not, Bill. Reltsur will be back soon, an' if we're not here, he'll raise Jim Henry. But if you can keep that loose tongue of yors still fer a while, I'm goin' to sleep. G'night."

The boys heard a body move restlessly about, as though trying to find a comfortable spot for repose. Roy glanced back. At his elbow Bug Eye crouched, gun out and raised. Close to him stood Gus and Nick.

"Teddy!" Roy whispered. "Get along side of me — like this. When I yell, we both jump together. You fellows follow. Ready?"

There was no need to answer. Roy saw his brother's face twitching eagerly, saw the shoulders hunched, the neck craned forward.

"Ye-o-o-w!"

"Get 'em, boys! Knock' em cold, if you have to, but get 'em!"

There was a fierce, sudden rush! Yells! Shouts!

"Hey! what in thunder's this? Hey, you, take that gun outen my mouth!"

"They got us, Bill! Ouch, that's my nose! All right! You win! Only let up, fer Pete's sake!"

A short, desperate scuffle followed. The dull thud of a few blows, and Bill and his companion were sitting stupidly on the ground, stripped of their guns, the moon shining on two very much astounded cattle-rustlers who shook their heads in a dazed manner.

"If we had knowd you was goin' to roughhouse," Bill began in an aggrieved tone, "Sam an' me would've —"

"Nick —" Roy spoke sharply — "you stay here and watch these men! If they give you any trouble, shoot!"

"With pleasure!" Nick responded, grinning. "But at present they seem to be perfectly comfortable. Hey, gents?"

The one called Sam looked up dubiously. "Well, I got a pack of cards an' if yore so inclined, we might —"

Neither Teddy nor Roy heard the rest, for they, followed by Gus and Bug Eye, were running along the trail. Ahead of them they made out a dark splotch against the stone walls. As they came closer they saw that it was an entrance to a cavern.

"The Caves!" Teddy yelled, careless of consequences. "Belle! Ethel! Are you there? Belle!"

"Teddy!"

A figure ran from the opening of the cavern and toward him. The next moment it had cast itself into his arms.

"Oh, Teddy! Roy! We thought you'd never come! Three days we were kept in there! Three days!" Belle was sobbing openly now, catching at Roy and Teddy by turns and kissing them. But in a moment she regained something of her composure, and called:

"Nell! Ethel! Come out! It's all right! The boys are here! They've found us!"

Then on that moonlit ledge was one of the strangest and happiest scenes in which the boys had ever taken part. Bug Eye cheered and Gus chuckled in that inimitable way of his, while the rest took turns congratulating each other. Especially did Nell and Ethel pay outrageous tribute to Roy and Teddy, insisting that they were:

"Oh, so much better than those old knights who rescued ladies from dungeons! And would they consent to sign their names in this little book, please?"

In the midst of all this merriment and hilarity, Clovita came to the doorway of the cave, wearing a wide grin. She did not seem at all disturbed at the turn affairs had taken. When the boys saw her they started back.

"The old woman we saw at the cabin! How did she get here? Why, we left her on the trail hours ago. She even talked to us! How —"

"She my sister — we twins," Clovita declared, grinning wider than ever. "You meet her, yes? She not so nice, maybe?"

"I'll tell a maverick she wasn't!" Roy exclaimed. "But never mind that now. You girls — you're all right? They gave you plenty to eat and drink?"

"We're fine," Ethel laughed happily. "But won't it feel great to be home again! The first thing I'm going to do is —"

She was interrupted by a yell, coming from the place they had captured the guards. Roy reached for his gun. Then he let out a roar of laughter as Nick called out:

"Hey, Roy, these two geezers won all my money playin' seven-up! Come down here quick, or they'll have my shirt! An' bring a new pack of cards! These are marked, or I'm a ring-tailed dodo-bird!"

CHAPTER XXV

THE MORNING JOY

"What a night *that* was!"

Teddy, turning on his pillow, observed his brother. The early afternoon sun was streaming through the windows of their bedroom at the ranch house of the X Bar X. From the yard came sounds of a missing motor, interrupted by:

"Now yore hittin' along, you ole puddle jumper. Hear that engine, Nick? Sweet, ain't she, since I put that new carburetor on? Baby, this here lead mule — Stall on me, will yuh! Consarn yore brake-bands, I'll blow yore piston rings clear to —"

"Bug Eye," Teddy said, grinning. "He's got his flivver out there. Reckon some one drove it over for him." The boy yawned, and stretched high.

Roy observed the ceiling complacently. He seemed perfectly content to lie there, and think — think of the many things that had happened not twenty hours ago. Last night they were in Thunder Canyon, at Sholo Caves. Now they were at home, in their own room, listening to Bug Eye's "Address to a Flivver."

Lazily, Roy recalled that ride out of the canyon with the three girls and the two prisoners on horses they had found picketed near the cave. Clovita had gone with them, and it was lucky she had, for she showed them a short cut to the other side of the canyon, where they had met Mr. Manley and his party. His joy at having Belle back safe and sound was tremendous, as well it might be, and on that long ride home his corncob pipe was never unlit for a second. His humor kept the party in constant gales of laughter, not even excepting the two captured rustlers, who seemed a bit relieved that the whole business was over. Nick promised to visit them in jail and try to win some of his money back.

They had found Reltsur where they had left him, leaning against a tree, muttering to himself. The wound Teddy had inflicted was severe, but not fatal, and Mr. Manley, at all times considerate, even to an enemy, insisted that he take his bronco, while he rode double with Teddy. Gus shook his head at this display of "misplaced sympathy," but, nevertheless, his admiration for his boss increased tenfold. In his own words, as he later described it to Rad Snell, "Mr. Manley is sure one white guy."

On their way out of the canyon they had passed the hut of the old woman, Clovita's sister. Here Clovita left them, Mr. Manley feeling that it would do no good to detain her. After all, she was but a tool in the hands of the outlaws. The last the boys saw of her she was beating on the door of the cabin with her bare fist, while within all was dark. Roy wondered vaguely if her sister had finally admitted her or whether she had to climb in a window.

The homecoming of the girls had been momentous. Mrs. Manley was waiting up, and with tears of joy in her eyes she embraced her daughter, and also Nell and Ethel.

"I knew you'd come to-night!" she exclaimed. "I just knew it! Belle, I prayed so hard for you all that you couldn't help being safe! And now I have a suggestion. Mrs. Moore and Norine want to make some tea and toast. What about it?"

The yell that had gone up was answer enough. And after the rustlers had been put in the bunk-house, with Sing Lung guarding them with a huge knife and a ferocious frown on his face that would have deceived any one who did not know him, the rescue party sat down to a late midnight supper.

Mr. Manley had bound Reltsur's arm up and quartered him with his companions, with Sing Lung as guard. As Roy, in bed, thought about this man a puzzled look came over his face.

"Say, Teddy," he remarked, sitting up and gazing out the window at Bug Eye and his precious flivver, "that's a funny name for any one to have."

"What?" Teddy opened his eyes stupidly. "You talkin' to me?"

"I say Reltsur is a mighty queer name."

"Yea?"

Silence, unbroken save for the slow breathing of the boys. Then,

"I got it!" Teddy yelled suddenly.

"You got what?"

"I know what Reltsur means! Jimminy, I just thought of it! Came to me like a flash. I was always quick like that. Fast on my feet, too. I remember one time —"

"Well, for the love of Pete, spill it! What does Reltsur mean?"

Teddy gazed at his brother, a grin on his face.

"Spell it backwards!"

"Spell it —" Roy stopped and looked thoughtful. "Let's see. R-u-s-t-l-e-r. Rustler! By jinks, Teddy, you're right! Rustler! Who'd have thought it? The crazy guy. Using a thing like that for a name! Golly, he must be cookoo. Must think he's a villain out of the middle ages. In those days a man would take for his name anything that —"

"You don't say!" Teddy interrupted, laughing. "Well, that's what Relt-sur means, all right. Let's get up and tell dad. Baby, that was some sleep! We got in about twelve, didn't we? From twelve until — let's see, one-thirty. Wow! I'm hungry! Let's go down and see Ethel and Nell, and then we eat."

As the boys descended the stairs, Teddy thought with a smile that but a few hours ago they weren't sure whether they would ever see the old ranch again. They had expected a fierce fight, and were ready for it. They knew those rustlers could shoot, and Teddy and Roy had resigned themselves to whatever might occur. Yet they had met no one but an old woman and two punchers who played cards with Nick Looker! Teddy laughed aloud as he recalled Nick's plaintive cry from the trail of Thunder Canyon:

"Hey, Roy, these two geezers won all my money playin' seven-up!"

Outside, in the yard, Bug Eye was surrounded by a crowd to whom he was explaining the mysteries of his new carburetor. Belle and Ethel were standing arm in arm, and Mr. Manley was chuckling gleefully at Bug Eye's attempt to show that a four-cylinder motor ran better when two of the cylinders refused to fire.

"She's supposed to do that!" he was insisting. "That's what this here doohickey is for — to con-serve gas! You see, yay, look who comes! Boys, you're just in time! Make way! Make way, you vassels — or something like that. What's the good word, boys?"

"Listen, and I'll give you the low-down," Roy laughed. "Dad, Teddy made a discovery — a stu-pen-dous discovery. He found out what Reltsur means!"

"He did, son? What is it?"

"Spell it backwards and you'll soon see!"

For a moment there was silence. Nick's head bobbed up and down, his tongue on his lower lip as he figured it to himself. Gus and Bug Eye struggled manfully, but had to wait until Mr. Manley shouted:

"Rustler! That's it, sure as shootin'! Teddy, you're a genius! It's rustler turned around!"

"I always thought that bozo was a little balmy," Pop Burns declared, when the matter was explained to him. "Now I know it! Snakes, it's a wonder he doesn't walk backwards! Huh! Rustler, hey? Guess he's had enough action for a while, anyhow. He can think up new names fer himself while he's sittin' in jail — an' if you take my advice, that won't be at Hawley, boss!"

With a laugh, Mr. Manley agreed. Then he glanced fondly at his two sons, who had, together with their friends, brought this Reltsur to justice and had rescued Belle and the others from his clutches.

But the ranch boys were to have other happenings, and the further adventures of Roy and Teddy will be told in the next volume, to be called: "The X Bar X Boys on Whirlpool River."

Teddy, leaning forward, whispered to Ethel. She nudged Belle and Nell, and, casually, the three girls walked away from the little group surrounding Bug Eye, who had continued his demonstration.

In a few moments the boys followed and met the girls near the corral. It was the work of but a few moments to saddle Flash and Star and three other ponies.

Softly they rode out of the yard. If any one saw them, they gave no sign. Once behind the corral Teddy leaped Flash forward.

"Let's go!" he yelled. "To that stump out there! See it? Come on!"

Over the prairie the riders swept. And as they left the ranch houses, there came to them a faint, far-off voice:

"Now this carburetor, she works on a funny system. First the gas condenses in here, ya see, an' the air is let in by this here doofunny — —"